Cutler's Chase

a John Cutler mystery

by Colin Conway

*For Bilbo, Tarsh, Cricket,
Daisy, Reba, Brisco, Shelby,
Emma, Ali, Rose, and Teddy*

"You were dead, you were sleeping the big sleep, you were not bothered by things like that, oil and water were the same as wind and air to you. You just slept the big sleep, not caring about the nastiness of how you died or where you fell."

- *The Big Sleep*/Raymond Chandler

Cutler's Chase

2005

Chapter 1

My eyes fluttered open, and I squinted against a light shining in my face. As I sat up, a hand grabbed my shoulder and pushed me to the ground. A voice said something I couldn't make out. I relented and lay back.

More voices now. These others seemed further away and happily yelled over the thumping bass line of Kanye West's "Gold Digger." The club, I thought, that's where I am. The music and chattering voices swirled nauseatingly inside my head.

What the hell happened?

"Easy," a male voice said. "Take it easy."

The light in my eyes seemed brighter as if it had moved closer.

"Are you okay?"

I waved at the light. "Get that outta my face."

"Relax," the voice said, and the bright light moved away. "We're only here to help."

A young police officer knelt next to me. He wore white latex gloves, and his name badge read *Delaney*. The flashlight he held pointed downward. "What happened?"

Pain cascaded over the right side of my face. "I don't remember." I turned and spat a glob of blood onto the concrete floor. Delaney straightened and stepped away.

I hacked, and it set off an explosion inside my head. Rolling over to my hands and knees, I sucked for air. Blood drooled from my mouth. I spat once more.

Officer Delaney again. "What's the last thing you remember?"

Dropping back to my butt, I said, "Working the floor."

While my tongue searched for broken teeth, I stole a glance around the bar. Music pounded from the speakers hanging from Club Royale's ceiling. Multi-colored lights flickered. People of all shapes, sizes, and colors danced without concern.

At the front door and nearer to me, several police officers interviewed a group of customers. Watching me intently from that group was Erika Taylor, a late-twenties black woman. She gave a small, concerned wave when we made eye contact.

"Hey," the cop said.

My tongue discovered a large gash on the inside of my cheek.

Delaney leaned over and spoke in the slow speech pattern reserved for foreigners. "Do you remember what happened?"

I pushed myself to a knee.

"Don't get up. Medics are on the way."

"I'm fine." Holding the wall for support, I made it to my feet.

"So, you were working the floor, and then woke up on it?"

"What can I say?"

Erika continued to watch from the edge of the crowd.

"Yeah," Delaney said and clicked off his flashlight. He slipped it into the thigh pocket of his pants. "What *can* you say? Wait here."

Erika hurried over then. "Are you—"

"Fine." It was the same thing I'd told the cop. I didn't feel that way, though.

She studied my head and grimaced.

I touched the right side of my face. Finding wetness, I pulled the fingers back and saw them covered in dark red. "How bad?"

"There's a gash. Not too long, but it's bleeding like hell."

I removed a crushed pack of Marlboros from my pocket. I fished around for a smokable cigarette. "Did you see what happened?"

Erika was a member of the club's waitstaff. She wore the requisite midriff shirt emblazoned with the club's logo. After a glance toward the cops, she said, "Croy Bradford."

"This was some sort of payback?"

"Maybe."

Bradford played for a local university and was the stereotypical farm boy. Tall, blond, thick in the chest, and thicker in the head. He was also a mean drunk. A couple of weeks prior, he tied one on and tried pulling one of the servers into a VIP room. Crazy, sometimes illegal, things happened in the VIP rooms but only when it's consensual. The server didn't want to go, but Bradford and his buddies were insistent.

After I told Bradford and his cronies to knock it off, we had a shoving match. His poor attitude ended his night. With the help of several other bouncers, I tossed the farm boy on the sidewalk—much to his embarrassment and the perverse joy of the assembled crowd waiting to get inside.

"That tells me who," I said, "not how."

Erika's gaze swept once more over the assembled cops. "He hit you with a beer bottle."

"From behind?"

"That's what I heard. I didn't see it."

Bradford stood close to six and a half feet tall, weighed in around two-fifty, and was now in his senior year of college. If he swung a bottle, there would have been a significant force behind it. I'm lucky my head was still attached.

Erika said, "You're lucky your head is still attached."

I eyed her, wondering if she could read my mind.

"What?"

"Where were the guys?"

"Right before you got hit, another fight started near the DJ. Don't you remember?"

"Sort of." The others had moved toward a donnybrook on the far side of the dance floor. "Interesting timing, that."

I pulled a crumpled cigarette from the pack and lit it. A deep inhale made me lightheaded, and the world tilted. I reached out for the wall, and Erika grabbed my arm.

"You okay?"

Bile rose in my throat, and the cigarette slipped from my fingers. Erika ground it out with her shoe.

Weakly, I asked, "Did you tell the police?"

She stared at me.

I looked over her shoulder. The cops were still talking, but it looked as if Delaney was starting to pull away.

"Isaiah," she said. Her younger brother was a running back on the same team. "He was here, too."

"So?"

"I missed Croy hitting you, but I saw Isaiah snatch the bottle from him. He smashed it on the floor on the way out."

My gaze drifted toward the front door. There appeared to be a pile of glass.

"Right."

"I'm sorry, John. I thought Isaiah had finally gotten his shit together."

"Doesn't seem that way."

"This is bad. It's inexcusable."

"What are you asking me to do?"

"Nothing. I just thought you should know."

I lifted my chin toward the group of people standing near the cops. "Somebody probably saw him."

"It's okay."

"One of the crew might have seen him, too."

"I know." Her face remained passive. "Never mind."

"What if I tell the cops what you told me?"

She looked down. "Then you tell them. It's okay."

"Did they ask what you saw?"

Erika didn't look up.

"Right." I absently dug in the pack of cigarettes again but stopped. I didn't need to feel any woozier. "Your brother and Bradford aren't welcome back here."

She nodded. "Thank you, John."

"Don't thank me. If I ever see Bradford—" I let the threat hang in the air. "Pass that message to your brother."

Erika nodded again.

Officer Delaney came back over. "Anything jog your memory?"

"No."

The cop pointed at a group I assumed were witnesses. "They say you got blindsided by a big white guy with a beer bottle."

"Look around. The club is full of big white boys with beer bottles. It's Spokane, for Christ's sake."

The officer frowned. "One of them thought he might be a ball player or something."

"News to me."

Delaney eyed Erika. "You?"

"I missed the whole thing." She pointed to the other side of the club. "I was over there."

"And no one has said anything?"

She shrugged. "Nu-uh."

The officer faced me once more. Even though he was young, his eyes were filled with the judgment many cops develop. I should know. I used to see it in the mirror.

"Why do you think he did it?" Delaney asked.

"No idea."

"Maybe you cut him off. Maybe you didn't let him in some other time. Maybe you kicked him out previously. You're not even willing to take a guess?"

Sirens from outside announced an approaching ambulance.

"Am I free to go?" I asked.

Delaney sighed heavily. "The medics should check you out."

Erika snaked her arm through mine. "I'll make sure he gets there."

The cop waved us toward the door.

Outside the bar, red and blue lights bounced off the neighboring buildings,

"I won't forget what you did for me," she said.

When the medics approached, Erika backed off. She listened to their initial questions about my injury then returned to the club.

Chapter 2

Two hours later, Deaconess Hospital discharged me with ten stitches in the side of my head. It wasn't a big cut, but head wounds bleed like hell. I had no idea how I would pay for the visit. Health insurance was a memory, a figment of my imagination, a socialist's dream. Maybe Bosco and the club would cover it since it was an injury sustained while working.

As I walked downtown, my head throbbed with each step. It wasn't yet two in the morning. The bars were still active, and their customers ran in and out of them like it was the most crucial duty they had in the world. For some, it probably was. To the young, Friday night was the king of the week. They either use it or lose it. They haven't realized yet there will always be another one. Or maybe I simply stopped caring about Fridays.

Walking the fifteen blocks to my apartment took twenty minutes. I usually enjoyed being out in the hot August evenings, but not tonight. My shirt stuck to me from a combination of sweat and undried blood. The nausea hadn't dissipated, and it felt like it would hang around until the morning.

At the Claremont Apartments, I punched in the code for the front door's security pad. When the lock clicked open, I entered. The combination lock gave the illusion of security, but anyone could watch and learn the simple code—it was the building's three-digit address. The property management company kept it simple so most of the drunks in the building wouldn't forget.

Outside the elevator, I pressed the flickering UP button. Occasionally, I take the stairs because it's about the only exercise I get anymore. My weight may not have been much more than when I left Seattle, but my stomach was softer, and my muscles were weaker. The occasional push-ups I did weren't enough to stave off the atrophy of my physique.

The elevator shuddered to a stop, and the doors opened with a grinding noise.

The inside of the box smelled like vomit, and my nausea intensified. I swallowed it back. My thumb pressed 6, and I waited for the doors to come together. When they finally closed, new graffiti greeted me. Every few days, someone would scrawl something across the light blue doors that the management team would cover up with a fresh paint coat.

FUCK The World! and the hoarse you road in on.

As I stared at the words and contemplated their misspelled philosophical relevance, the elevator climbed upward. The graffiti appeared to have started as a single-word commentary, and then two others contributed their insight. I was lost in thought when the elevator jerked to a stop and threw off my balance. I slammed into the wall, banged my elbow against the metal rail, then crashed to the rubber floor mat.

The doors squeaked open, revealing the sixth floor. Flickering fluorescent lights illuminated the hallway. I stood and stumbled out.

Loud music pounded from the apartment nearest the elevator. It sounded something like blenders, drills, and jigsaws running at the same time. Carefully, I shuffled to my apartment, running my hand along the wall to help keep me stable.

From inside apartment 617, I could hear a woman

yelling. Stopping for a moment, a habit from the days when I protected and served, I listened. Even though I couldn't make out her words, the conversation sounded one-sided, like she was on a telephone. With a shrug, I continued on my way.

At my door, I slipped my key into the lock.

Chapter 3

Banging and yelling in the hallway brought me out of dreamless sleep. My mouth tasted like crap, and bells clanged in my ears. I struggled upright in bed. I had slept in my clothes. The box fan in my apartment was off, and the air hung heavy and stale.

I stood as the hammering continued outside. It only took me a few steps to cross my apartment and open the door. Several heads popped out of the other units lining the hallway.

Down the way, a large man in a leather jacket battered his fist against a door. The size of his shoulders and chest reminded me of those steroid freaks who pretend that they're wrestlers. He had long black hair, and stubble covered his face.

"Open up," he hollered and kicked the bottom of the door. He was making a hell of a racket. "You bitch!"

I moved into the hallway for a better look. My motion caught his eye, and he turned in my direction. "The fuck you looking at? Go back inside."

Last year, I fought a man roughly the same size. I'm a decent fighter, but that altercation didn't go well for me. After last night, I wasn't in the mood to provoke this guy. When I didn't respond to his question, he returned to kicking the door.

"Open up!"

"Go away," a woman screamed.

Not feeling my finest or my bravest, I turned to go into my apartment. But a hand rested on my shoulder and stopped me. I glanced at Peyton Meyers, the retired Marine who lived diagonally across the hall.

"Hey, Slick."

Even though Peyton was in his late fifties, he always appeared ready for active duty. He wore his usual attire—a gray t-shirt, black cargo pants, and black combat boots.

He squinted. "Jesus. Who did you murder?" Peyton pulled at my shirt. "Is all that blood yours?" He then examined the stitches in the side of my head. I had removed the bandage covering them before going to bed. "The hell happened?"

"Got hit with a bottle."

The banging and yelling down the hall continued.

Peyton flashed a disapproving look in the large man's direction then turned back to me. "Are you gonna live?"

"I think so."

The woman screamed from inside her apartment. "Go away, Houston!"

Peyton's face scrunched as he considered the scene down the hall. He eyed me again. "You sure you're okay?"

"According to the doctor."

Another bang came from down the hall, followed by more pleading from the woman.

Peyton motioned down the hallway. "Then can we do something about this?"

"What do you mean we?"

"I mean the two grown men standing around holding their junk while that animal is down there disturbing the peace."

Houston kicked the door. "Let me in!"

"Go!" the woman screamed.

"Take your dog," I said.

Peyton smirked. "I don't want the dog to bite that turd

and catch a dirty disease."

"What about me?"

There was more kicking and screaming from down the hall.

The former Marine slapped me with the back of his hand. "You'll heal. Look how good your head is coming along. C'mon."

I glanced down at my bare feet. "Let me get some shoes."

"Pansy."

"I don't think I'm in any condition—"

"You'll be fine." Peyton turned and hollered down the hall, "Hey! Mouth breather!"

"Wait," I said.

Houston spun in our direction. "What'd you call me?" His voice echoed through the hallway.

Peyton patted my shoulder, "My friend says you need to shut your cock garage."

"My what?"

The former Marine pumped his hand in and out near his mouth then pointed to the big man.

It took a moment for Houston to understand Peyton's implication. When he did, his eyes widened.

Peyton put his hand on my shoulder. "That's what my friend thinks of you."

Houston grunted and ran in our direction.

The former Marine slapped my back. "Buckle up, buttercup."

The big man's shoes slapped the hallway's linoleum floor while he ran. As he neared, he hunched like a sack-hungry linebacker. I stepped into him and twisted, using his force to turn him. We slammed into the floor together with him on the bottom. The drop didn't startle him as I'd hoped, and the fight was on.

Houston punched upward, and I tucked my chin. I kept the injured side of my head turned away to protect my stitches. I straddled his chest and hit him. He was a brawler and knew how to fight from the bottom. My blows deflected off his shoulders as he kept moving his head. He snapped punches upward. Several caught me in the forehead. Arm length was to his advantage. We traded strikes for several crazy moments until he seized up.

"Gah—" he exclaimed, and his eyes widened. He bucked wildly like a bull trying to throw a cowboy. I jumped off and backpedaled until I bumped into a wall.

Peyton grinned. "A solid boot to the jimmies stops 'em every time."

Houston rolled to his side and curled into a fetal position. He cupped himself with both hands.

The former Marine leaned over the big man. "Not so tough now, are you?"

From down the hall, footsteps pounded the floor. Three police officers rounded the corner and trotted in our direction. Each of them wore dark blue uniforms and black leather gloves that stood in stark contrast to their short sleeves.

The first officer, an intense guy with alert eyes, stopped a few feet away from us. His silver nametag read *Morgan*. He pointed at the big man on the floor. "What happened?"

Peyton thumbed in my direction. "Slick had to be a hero."

The other two officers moved toward me when a woman yelled from down the hall. "Not him. The one on the ground." She leaned partially out from her apartment. Her long dark hair was disheveled. "I was the one that called."

Morgan stepped back and let the other officers cuff Houston. When they finished, they lifted the large man to his feet and escorted him down the hall. As they passed the woman's apartment, Houston hollered, "I'll kill you!"

Morgan laughed. "I love when they help write the report." His brow furrowed, and he studied my shirt. "Is that blood?"

"From last night. I bounce at Club Royale."

"You didn't change?"

"I fell asleep."

The officer eyed Peyton, who only shrugged in return.

Morgan's gaze returned to me. "So this guy," he thumbed down the hall, "created a disturbance, and you kicked his ass?"

"Not me." I lifted my chin toward Peyton. "Him. The old man started in with his Marine stories, and the big guy wanted to fight."

Morgan raised an eyebrow. "You really in the Corps?"

"Twenty-two years. Retired." Peyton turned his forearm to reveal a faded USMC tattoo.

Morgan performed the same action and showed a similar tattoo.

The older man kicked his head back and bellowed, "Hooah."

"Great," I said, "now, there's two of you."

The officer patted Peyton's shoulder. "I need your names and stories for the report."

We gave our information, which he recorded into his notebook. Then we quickly told our side of things. Afterward, the officer headed toward apartment 617.

Alone now, Peyton eyed my stitches. The way he looked reminded me of Clint Eastwood in *Heartbreak Ridge.* "You do look like hell."

"Have you seen a mirror lately? And what was that crap about getting me into a fight?"

He shrugged. "I thought it would be more fun than reading the newspaper. It's been kinda dull around here."

"You're weird."

"So I've heard."

I stepped into my apartment.

"Hey," he said. "Swing by for a beer later?"

"Maybe."

"Don't be a pansy."

"Yeah, okay." I shut the door.

Another "Hooah" came from the hallway.

Chapter 4

After a shower, I walked down the hall and knocked on apartment 617. I wanted to check on the woman who lived there. When she didn't answer, I went to Peyton's.

We lived at the end of the hallway and near the window that overlooked the southern portion of downtown. It was also the access point to the fire escape. I knocked.

A voice boomed from inside the apartment. "Whozzit?"

"Cutler."

The door swung open. "Slick, why don't you just walk in?"

I pointed at a German Shepherd sitting in the middle of the room. It appeared as if he was sizing me up for his next meal. "He might eat me."

Peyton closed the door behind me then headed for the kitchen. "That dog ain't gonna eat you. You're one of the good guys."

"How does *he* know that?"

"I told him, and he doesn't forget. He's smarter than most people."

Peyton handed me a Budweiser. I sat in a chair, and the dog walked over.

"Corporal," Peyton said, "Parade rest."

The dog immediately sat. His big, sloppy tongue hung from his mouth. I ran my fingers over his head.

"Hey," I said with my hand in the Corporal's fur, "why didn't you name him Colonel or Major or something fancy like that?"

"Name him after an officer? You puke. You'd like that,

wouldn't you? I'd never name a dog after some Annapolis candy-ass."

"Then why not name him Sergeant. Or at least Sarge? Give the guy some rank."

"A corporal has rank," Peyton muttered. He sipped his beer. His voice lowered as he continued as if filled with some remorse. "He's my second Shepherd. The first was Private."

"And a corporal follows a private in rank."

The older man tipped his beer at me. "Not bad for a civilian."

Corporals existed in the police department—a quasi-military organization but now didn't seem the time for that discussion.

Peyton continued. "I had Private for ten years before his hip dysplasia got so bad that I had to put him down." He sighed heavily. "When I decided to get another dog, I figured Corporal was as good a name as any."

"The next one will be Sergeant?"

Peyton set his beer on the floor. "This one is the last. He's four years old. I figure another six or so years with him is what I've got. I'm not looking forward to putting another dog down. When that happens, I'm done. I'll never go through it again. There's been enough death in my life."

Something passed through Peyton's eyes. He was a career Marine, so there had to have been a time or two when he saw death in that line of work, but he never talked about anything close to it. The stories he told were either funny or action oriented. If I were to believe Peyton's version of the Marines, death never touched them. He once had a family he mentioned only in passing. All he said was they had died several years ago. I don't know how it happened. He never shared it, and I didn't feel it my place to inquire.

Motioning toward my beer, he asked, "Want to shoot some stick later?"

"No, thanks."

"You always turn me down. Don't like pool?"

"Was never any good at it."

"Don't have to be good at it to have some fun."

"Maybe another day. I'm working tonight."

He pointed at my stitches. "Going back for more?"

"Got no choice. It's my job."

Peyton laughed. "Hell, Slick, maybe you could've been a Marine."

Chapter 5

"No, no, no!"

I was barely through the door when Bosco, Club Royale's owner, shook his head and waved his arms. He hurried toward me.

"Not you," he said in his thick accent. "Not tonight."

Bosco was his last name. I'd heard his first once, but no one outside his home country could pronounce it. Many immigrants come into the country and adopt a new American first name just to fit in. He was lucky that his last was so easy to master. Around town and in the industry, he was simply known as Bosco.

He wore a tight black t-shirt over his barrel chest, and a simple, silver chain hung around his neck. His black slacks looked new and recently pressed. Bosco took pride in his appearance. He also had pride that he owned a nightclub less than ten years after coming to America.

The club wasn't open yet. Various staff members actively cleaned and prepped for the upcoming night.

"What are you talking about?" I asked.

"Stitches and bruises." Bosco pointed at my head. Some bruising was starting to show along the side of my face. "Bad for business."

"I got tagged working for you."

"That happened because you were not paying attention."

I frowned. "It's Saturday night."

"So?"

"If I don't work, I don't get paid."

He folded his arms. "That is life."

"If I don't get paid, I'm going somewhere else. Who will run security for you?"

Bosco scowled.

"You're not the easiest guy to work for."

He rubbed his face before surreptitiously glancing at the other guys on the security team who were just arriving. He grabbed my elbow and walked me to the door. "Take tonight off," he whispered. "I will pay. Come back on Monday. We will see what your face looks like then."

"My face is fine. It's my head that's injured."

Bosco scrunched his nose. "Your face is not fine, but that is good for business." He barked a laugh, patted my shoulder once, then hurried off to elsewhere in the club.

***

I stopped at the corner and removed a cell phone from my pocket. I wasn't sure how many minutes I had left on the thing, but it wouldn't be a long call.

She answered after the third ring. "Hi, this is Tanya."

"Hey. I got the night off."

"Oh."

"Is this a bad time?"

"Sort of," Tanya said. "Can I call you back later?"

Even though she couldn't see it, I shrugged. "Don't worry about it."

"That sounds great."

"If you want." Another shrug she couldn't see. "You know where I live."

"Okay, thanks." She hung up.

I snapped the phone closed.

Chapter 6

The digital clock showed 12:37 a.m. I blinked at the red lights amid a soft knocking on my door. The room was warm even though the box fan stuck in the open window whirred loudly. My blankets were in a pile on the floor.

With a grunt, I sat upright as the light tapping continued. I padded to the door and opened it. Tanya wore a tight black blouse, blue jeans, and strapless high heels. Her eyes were glassy from drinking, and she held a bottle of red wine in her hand.

She whispered throatily, "You called?"

I stepped back and let her in. With a swipe of her arm, she flicked on the lights as she walked by. After closing the door, I turned around.

Her eyes widened. "What happened?" She touched my head, then my cheek where the bruising had crept.

"Got jumped at the club."

"I'd hate to see the other guy." She appraised my wound once more before going into the kitchen. She knew where the wine opener was and expertly worked the cork free from the bottle she'd brought. Afterward, she collected a couple of coffee mugs from my cabinet. "You need appropriate glassware."

"It's not in the budget."

"I'll get them for you."

"The mugs work fine."

"Says you." She poured us both a cup of what was sure to be an expensive blend. "I'm sorry I couldn't talk earlier, but I was having dinner with my sister." Her sister disapproved of how Tanya lived her life. That was, of course, if she was indeed having dinner with her sibling. It might have been code for something else.

When she was in high school, Tanya was runner-up for Miss Teen Washington. She never finished that well in the competition for Miss Washington. Nowadays, she was the former Mrs. Donald Robertson, the ex-wife of one of the wealthiest men in town. She was intelligent, beautiful, and bored. Tanya was careening her way to forty in neither a graceful nor healthy manner. I was one of those things contributing to that lack of elegance.

She shimmied her way across the room while holding the two coffee mugs. Tanya handed me one and took a sip of hers. "It's a Bordeaux."

I sipped the wine. "How's your sister?"

"Hmmm?" Tanya swayed her hips to some non-existent music.

We met at Club Royale almost ten months ago. She came in with a few friends, apparently on the hunt for some trouble. We chatted a bit, but I knew better than to tangle with a drunk, recently divorced woman.

Tanya came back the next week and reintroduced herself when she paid the cover. Through the evening, she spent most of the time hanging around the door and flirting. By the end of the night, she told me she wanted to see me after my shift. She remained sober throughout, so I walked her over to my apartment. My misgivings about getting involved with a recently divorced drunk woman didn't seem to extend to them when they were sober. Besides, I figured once she saw where I lived, she would become disinterested.

What she got from me I never quite figured out. I was low rent. From her perfect eyelashes to her pedicured toes, she exuded money. I suspected she saw other guys. That's probably where she was earlier when she said she was with her sister. I wanted to ask, but what we had didn't allow it. My purpose was never to rise to boyfriend status.

Tanya was the only woman I saw. It wasn't love, though. I didn't pretend it to be. The last time I said that word to a woman resulted in me getting hurt. Being with Tanya this way suited my life. I wasn't interested in committing to anyone.

She swayed before kicking her mug back. When Tanya finished its contents, she smiled with slightly purple lips. "Do you like it?"

"It's good."

"It better be good." She started humming as she kicked off her heels then unbuttoned her jeans. "Better be good," she repeated in a sing-song way. She pointed at me then continued humming.

Tanya pushed her pants to the floor. She wasn't wearing any underwear. A bit clumsy due to the alcohol, she attempted to step out of the puddled denim. She stumbled with her pants around one ankle, and the humming stopped. "Oops." An embarrassed giggle escaped before she pulled the black shirt over her head.

She leaned over and kissed me. She smelled freshly washed. "Good or bad?"

I touched her face. "Your choice."

Tanya returned to the kitchen and poured herself another mug of Bordeaux. On her way back, she slipped back into her heels. It only took a couple of gulps for her to finish the mug's contents. She set it on the coffee table. "Okay, John Cutler." Her hip thrust to the side. "I've been a naughty girl."

***

An hour later, she tiptoed into the bathroom. The shower started.

I slipped on my running shorts and lay back on the bed. Briefly, I thought about turning around the box fan to blow in the cool night air, but I was too tired to move. Tanya's motivation after all the wine and whatever else she had to drink amazed me.

Several minutes passed before she strode out of the bathroom smelling like Irish Spring.

"You can stay the night," I said. It was a hollow offer. She never spent the night, and I didn't really want her to. It was a polite thing people say after doing what we did.

"Someday," she lied. "But not tonight."

I rolled over to my side and watched her dress. She didn't have a job, a family, or a husband to rush home for. Instead, she was hurrying away from me or whatever I represented. Was it where I lived? Was it my current income level? Was it my lack of earning potential?

It wasn't the first time I had those thoughts. I'm sure it wouldn't be the last.

Tanya zipped her jeans before leaning over to kiss my forehead lightly. "Thank you for calling." She pulled the door closed behind her.

It wasn't love, I reminded myself.

Sleep eluded me for some time after that.

Chapter 7

"I screwed up, Slick."

Peyton sat on the edge of my couch with his arms crossed over his chest. He tucked his hands into his armpits. He lowered his head.

"How so?" I asked.

He muttered something only he could hear.

"Hey, man. Talk to me."

Peyton flopped backward on the couch and closed his eyes. It was three in the afternoon when he showed up at my door. A couple of minutes had passed since then, and he remained pale and shaking.

The fan in the window spun noisily, yet the apartment still felt stuffy.

"Need a beer or something?" I asked.

With his eyes still shut, he nodded.

From the refrigerator, I fetched us two cans. I popped his open and handed it to him. When Peyton took his beer, I noticed his knuckles were raw and bloody.

He drew deeply from the can. "Thanks."

I silently saluted him with my unopened beer.

Peyton rolled his can back and forth between his hands. After a minute, he stopped and looked at me. "We haven't talked about my wife and daughter."

I leaned against the kitchen counter. "No."

He took a large pull from his beer before speaking again. "Connie and I got married when we were twenty-one. I was three years into the Corps by then. Connie decided that it was better to marry me than to kick me free." He smiled at the memory. "We had a daughter a year later that we named Diana. After some character in a book that Connie liked. Our baby was beautiful, just like her mother."

He lifted the can but stopped short of taking another drink. "By the time I left the Corps, my mom and dad had died. I don't have any brothers or sisters. Was never close to any aunts or uncles. I had a lot of friends through the years, but I never got close to anyone except my girls. After I retired, we moved back to Montana, where I grew up." He frowned. "It was stupid to move there, I guess. Neither of us had a job waiting, and the school systems weren't much better than southern California, where I finished my tour, but I didn't have any ambitions to do anything except grow old with Connie. Missoula seemed as good a place as any."

Peyton set the can on the table then leaned back on the couch. "One weekend, the girls went to see some movie starring that Meg Ryan gal. You know who I'm talking about? Diana was still with us. She'd just finished another year at the university. Every couple of weeks, they'd do a mother-daughter outing that left me puttering around the house or hanging at the bar with a couple of the locals. That's what I was doing when they went out, having a beer and listening to music."

His gaze drifted to the ceiling, and he fell silent for some time.

The whirring box fan filled the silence.

When Peyton finally lowered his gaze to me, his voice wavered. "They were driving back from the theater when it happened." He swallowed with some difficulty then wiped his face. "An asshole in a Camaro t-boned them on Diana's side of the car. He blew through a red light without hitting the brakes." He punched a fist into an open palm. "Diana died immediately. At least, that's what the cops said. Connie wasn't so lucky."

Peyton shuddered but continued his story. "It took her three days to die. She was busted up bad." He angrily wiped at his eyes. "Massive head trauma. She wouldn't have lived a day without all the equipment that she was hooked up to. Were the extra days worth it?"

He looked at my door. No one had knocked. I wondered if he was thinking about leaving.

"That was fifteen years ago." His hand dragged from his chin down his neck. "Fifteen years. Not a day goes by that I don't think about Wayne Jeremiah Sadler."

I leaned forward and set down my unopened beer.

"Twenty-one years old," Peyton said. "The lucky prick wasn't wearing a seatbelt. Didn't go through the windshield. Didn't eat the steering wheel. Didn't break a leg." Peyton's lips trembled. "That little— Only broke his nose and—" He lifted his hand and rotated it. "—his wrist. My wife and daughter died, and all he got was a scratch." Peyton slammed a fist onto his leg. "A fucking scratch."

"What happened to Sadler after?"

Peyton swiped his hand over his mouth and tried to compose himself. He took a deep breath, held for a count of three, then exhaled. "The cops arrested him. They gave him a breath test. He registered point two-three. That didn't mean anything to me at the time, but the detective told me it was three times the legal limit. Three times! Can you believe that?"

I shook my head, even though I had no problem believing it. I'd seen similar instances when I was on the job.

"They charged Sadler for killing Diana and Connie. Vehicular homicide, they called it. Two counts. They had a hearing, and the judge set his bail at a hundred grand. That's all. That's what my family was worth!" Peyton took a swig of his beer then wiped his mouth with the back of his hand. "His parents paid the bail just like that." He snapped his fingers sharply. "Guy spent less than three days in jail. That's it."

"What do you mean, *that's it*?"

"He ran."

"To where?"

Peyton shrugged. "Who knows? The cops couldn't find him. The U.S. Marshals couldn't find him. He just… disappeared."

"The parents didn't have any idea?"

"As far as they were concerned, their baby boy was getting railroaded by the judicial system. They probably helped him flee."

"What about the bail bondsman?"

"Weren't you listening, Slick? They didn't use a bondsman. They posted cash—straight up."

"A hundred grand." I whistled.

Had the parents used a bondsman, they would have only put down a small portion of the bail. Typically, this percentage would be pledged along with an asset of higher value. When Sadler ran, the hypothetical bondsman would have been out his ninety percent, but he could go after the parents' listed asset for the outstanding amount. The bondsman could also go after Sadler, and if he found the man, he could bring him back to the court and recover the posted bail.

The parents posting the total amount of bail meant two things. One less person would search for their son in the event he ran. And they gave him a hundred-thousand-dollar head start.

"The cops," Peyton said, "tried to lean on the parents, but they denied everything. You know how it is. I mean, as long as they stood by their story, how could anyone prove anything? The cops and the feds still have him on their wanted list. I check now and then. There were initial rumors that he ran to Canada or France or some other liberal country. Nobody heard nothing. Sadler just vanished. Turned to vapor." He wriggled his fingers. "And me—I was left with no family. That's why I left Missoula. I couldn't stand the memories no more."

Peyton grabbed his beer and kicked it back. He waggled the empty can and set it on the table.

"Another?" I pushed my unopened can toward him.

He shook his head.

"So, how's this got to do with you screwing up?"

"I was on my way back from shooting stick with Deacon—" He glanced up. "I've told you about him?"

I nodded. Peyton never came out and said it, but I got the feeling that Deacon was connected with Spokane's criminal underworld. Peyton often played pool with the guy. It was one of the few things he seemed to look forward to.

"I was feeling good after taking the man for five bucks." A sad smile crossed his face. "That may not sound like a lot, but we don't play for much. I should have known something bad was on the way when God let me win. That's when I saw him."

"Who?" I asked, but I already knew the answer.

"Wayne Jeremiah Sadler." Peyton's voice was almost a whisper. "Standing in the alley next to that high-end pizza joint. You know the one? Just talking on his cell phone without a care in the world. I didn't know it was him at first. I walked by and even smiled. Imagine that? Nodding and grinning like a goddamned citizen at the man who killed my family. All the prick did in return was raise a pinky." He mimed the action. "You know, I might not have taken a second look at him if he had simply nodded back. But that stupid pinky," he mimed the action again, "so fucking arrogant. I had to take another look."

Peyton grabbed the empty beer can from the table. With his hands on the top and bottom, he twisted it in opposite directions. The aluminum noisily crumpled into a compressed state. It wasn't hard to guess what he was thinking.

He continued. "He was older, of course. A little heavier. Shit, the last time I saw him was fifteen years ago. I already told you that, didn't I? Sorry. I can't tell you how many times I've looked at his picture over the years. I'm not sure if he realized who I was, but he turned away. Didn't stop him from continuing his phone conversation, though."

"What did you do?"

"I called out his name. 'Wayne,' I said. And wouldn't you know it? He looked back. When our eyes met, well, that's when I knew for sure."

Peyton continued to press the aluminum can into a smaller package. His face reddened from the exertion. When he couldn't get it any smaller, he tossed it onto the table. He wiped the leftover wetness from his hands.

"I can promise you this, Slick, that boy never expected to see me again. It was like he saw a ghost. He tried to run, but I latched onto him and took him to the ground. He fought back, but I beat him as if my life depended on it. The boy didn't have a chance." Peyton scrunched his face into an odd expression. "Isn't that weird? I keep calling him a boy, but he's probably thirty-six now. Near your age." Peyton's face relaxed. "I'm not sorry for what I did, though."

Afraid of where his story might be leading, I folded my arms.

"I hit him until he passed out. Then I grabbed his neck." His eyes stared past me and were distant. "I was going to strangle that bastard—swear to God. It would have been the right thing to do, too. Maybe not New Testament, but surely Old Testament. An eye for an eye. After what he did, I'd risk my soul to find out. It doesn't matter now, though, because it never happened." He remorsefully shook his head. "A couple of ladies walked by the alley. Imagine what they saw. Me on top of the kid. My hands around his throat. They screamed bloody murder." He looked away. "Hearing them, I panicked. So stupid. I jumped and ran. Like a goddamned idiot."

"It was a natural reaction. Things got out of control."

His eyes hardened as they returned to me. "Not for me." Tapping his chest now. "Not for me! I'm a Marine. I've killed for God and country. I can't sleep a whole night anymore without men popping into my dreams. I pulled Marines out of firefights without so much a moment of hesitation, but two gray hairs scream at me, and I run like a frightened schoolboy." Tears welled in his eyes. "What does that make me?"

I ignored the question because he would never accept my answer.

"I should have stayed there. I caught him, Slick, something that the cops and the Feds couldn't do. The little bastard was in my hands." He stared at his empty palms. "And I got scared away by two old women."

"What happened after you left the alley?"

Peyton ground his palms against one another. "I hid at the Satellite."

"For how long?"

"Until I got enough guts to go back looking for him."

"Let me guess."

He nodded once. "Gone."

I thought about Peyton's situation. He should have held on to Sadler and let the cops come. Even if he were arrested for assault, a reasonable defense attorney, even a modest one, likely would have gotten Peyton's charge dismissed or reduced due to the history the two men shared. Then the police would have gotten Sadler, and he would be awaiting extradition to Montana for a trial now fifteen years past due. Instead, the wanted man had vanished.

"You're sure he remembered you?" I asked.

"If he didn't at first, he does now. I yelled Connie and Diana's names while beating him." Peyton's eyes traveled around the small apartment before returning to me. "What should I do?"

"What do you want to do?"

His eyes narrowed. "Are you a psychiatrist now?"

"No," I said. "But I doubt the cops will show up at your door. You need a victim for assault charges. No victim, no crime. Sadler won't report the assault because he'd get snatched on his warrant."

"You think I'm worried about getting arrested?" His voice rose with anger. "I'd gladly go to jail if it meant that piece of shit got his."

I patted the air with a hand. "I hear you but working yourself up isn't going to help anyone. Take Corporal for a long walk and forget about it."

"Forget about it?" His tone was sharp.

"Wrong choice of words. Don't forget Sadler or what

he did but let go of the incident in the alley. It happened, and it's over."

He smiled weakly. "Yeah. All right." He picked up the crushed can and fiddled with it. "Should I call the cops and tell them I saw him?"

"You should at least let them know he's in town. Maybe they could start looking for him. Being Sunday afternoon, if you call today, you'll either report it to an operator, or they'll send a patrolman out. If you wait until tomorrow and go into the station, you can ask to speak face-to-face with a detective or shift supervisor, maybe get a little more attention."

"What would you do?"

"I'm biased. You know my history."

He nodded. "What's the downside of reporting it?"

"The only one I see is if they catch him quickly, he'll be all busted up from the number you did on him. He could file an assault report and make it, so you'll have to defend yourself in court. But you don't care about that."

"No, I don't."

"Then you have your answer."

"Yeah, okay." Peyton stood and walked to the door. "Are you working tonight?"

"No."

"Drop by and see me. I'll show you some pictures of my family."

Chapter 8

After a nap, I showered and went for a walk. It was half-past six when I made it to Riverfront Park and sat on the grass across from the Opera House. A flock of ducks waddled along the muddy edge of the Spokane River before moving into the water.

Except for a young couple further up the hill, I was alone in my area of the park. The ducks now paddled, dipped, and dove under the water. Their movements seemed playful and became almost hypnotic. My mind soon drifted to my daughter, Erin.

I imagined losing her in the way Peyton lost his. Thoughts of remorse, revenge, and anger bounced about my consciousness. I'd hardly had Erin in my life, but I would want to kill anyone who took her from me. How had Peyton dealt with that anger all these years?

Leaning back on my elbows, I shifted my position. One duck appeared to take notice of my movement and circled several times near the water's edge. Eventually, it paddled further away.

Erin's mother, Maria, and I were never married. We never even lived together. Erin might have been the result of a short-term, ill-advised relationship, but she wasn't a mistake. Maria made sure of that. I'm thankful there was at least one level-headed person in the early days of that scenario.

The ducks banded together and moved further down the river. A wave of melancholy washed over me as the brightly colored flock moved along.

Child support payments and birthday cards don't make for a great father, but it was more than mine ever did. It was too low of a bar to clear to start patting myself on the back.

Sitting upright, I wiped the grass from my hands. It had been a while since I wrote Erin a letter. That wouldn't be a terrible way to spend the night.

***

When I returned to the apartment building, rock and roll music blasted from the apartment nearest the elevator. I couldn't remember the name of the song, but it was an old one that I'd heard somewhere before. The hallway smelled of floor wax, but there wasn't a fresh sheen to go along with it.

Passing by apartment 617, I paused. I lifted my hand to knock but didn't. Leave it alone, I thought. This isn't your fight.

Even without the knock, the door opened slightly. A thin brass chain stopped it from swinging all the way. A portion of a Hispanic woman's face appeared in the opening. Her dark hair fell around her shoulder, and light bruising surrounded her left eye. "Yes?"

I motioned down the hall. "I'm in six-three-three."

The door seemed to move slightly forward as if she were preparing to close it.

"Well," I said, suddenly feeling silly for standing there, "I wanted to see if you were okay after yesterday morning."

The woman considered me with some suspicion. "I'm fine."

"Okay," I said. "That's good."

I glanced in both directions. "Well, take care."
She closed the door.

***

On Peyton's apartment door was a note—*Slick, went to shoot pool. Come and find me if you want that beer*. From inside, I could hear Corporal moving about.

After entering my apartment, I went to the window. The evening sun hung almost reluctantly above the horizon. Across the way, a train arrived as a bus left the combined Amtrak and Greyhound bus station. People came and went. I imagined some came to Spokane for a better life while others fled the city for the same reason. The flow of bodies depressed me.

With thoughts of my daughter heavy on my heart, I spent the rest of the evening listening to the radio and writing her a letter.

Chapter 9

The red six announced its morning presence with a mocking glare. I clicked off the alarm and rolled out of bed. The temporary employment service I used to supplement my income had me scheduled with a full-day gig. Morris Ford City was preparing for its annual summer sale and needed drivers. They wanted a couple of hundred cars from their lots in downtown, north Spokane, and Spokane Valley shuttled to the fairgrounds. I was supposed to be at their downtown location by seven.

A shower and shave made me presentable. Using the cracked mirror, I ruffled the hair along the side of my head until it mostly hid the stitches. The bruising down my ear and cheek wasn't as bad as I thought. Maybe that was because I'd grown used to it.

Once dressed, I brewed a small pot of coffee and toasted two pieces of bread. I filled a used Styrofoam cup, buttered the toast, and carried them with me as I left my apartment. In the hallway, I saw that the note on Peyton's door was gone.

It was only a short walk to the downtown car lot, so I left my truck parked. The cool summer morning seemed a blessing as I strolled and ate.

I'd been arguing with myself recently about the temporary employment jobs. When I first moved to Spokane several years ago, the temp work provided a sort of free-floating existence. I wanted to drop out of society without going completely homeless. Not knowing where my next paycheck was coming from offered that experience in spades. Since then, I picked up the permanent gig at Club Royale. That was steady, if mostly mindless, work.

Over the past six months, a desire to do something more simmered in my gut. I was sensible enough to know I could never go back into law enforcement, not after how my career ended in Seattle. And even if I could, I'm not sure I would want to pursue it. Being a cop left a bad taste in my mouth. But I also was realistic enough to know that a Monday through Friday, eight-hour-a-day job didn't hold much appeal.

The idea that bubbled could be traced to two events.

A month ago, I helped an associate of a friend from the club find his stolen car. In the end, the automobile wasn't what the whole mess was about. It was the four laptop computers and the briefcase filled with counterfeit credit cards in the trunk. That messed with my morality a bit, but I rationalized it away by telling myself I didn't wear a badge anymore. Mine wasn't to uphold the law. It was to make ends meet. And the associate paid me enough to soothe my injured integrity.

The other event happened last fall. I returned to Seattle when a former girlfriend called. She wound up dead before I could help. Then I worked my way through a quagmire to find her killer. By the end of it all, four others were dead. Occasionally, I dealt with the remorse from that fiasco, but the experience let me believe I could do some sort of investigative work.

Thinking about investigating as a career left me feeling odd. It reminded me of police work—something that brought out the worst in me. However, it was something I might be good at which produced a strange sense of hope. It wasn't a thing I could worry about today, though. There were more pressing matters.

Before I made it to the dealership, I stopped at a mailbox to deposit Erin's letter.

***

It was almost seven in the evening when I left the downtown dealership and headed back to my apartment. Moving the cars went smoothly, but I was happy to be out from behind a steering wheel. Twelve hours in a car along the same one-way route is a mind-numbing way to spend a day. After a while, the vehicles all felt the same, especially since I never got to drive the flashier models—the younger guys all ran for them. The dealership wanted me back in a week to do it all again in reverse, bring the unsold cars back to the lot.

On the walk home, I stopped into Club Royale to see Bosco. The club owner strode out of the stockroom and raised an eyebrow when he saw me. I walked over to where he stood.

Bosco grabbed my chin and turned my head to inspect my injury.

"I'm ready to go," I said.

He let go of my chin. "Not tonight. Monday is bad business anyway. Your face scare away the little we get."

"It's my head that's hurt." I pointed at my temple. "Not my face."

Now, Bosco clapped my shoulder. "In my country, we have saying. 'Pity him a thousand glances.'"

I frowned.

"Is hard to translate, but it suits you."

My frown deepened, and Bosco barked a laugh. "Go home and be well. I still pay."

"About my medical bills—"

He nodded. "I pay my debts. All of them."

Erika approached. She wore faded jeans and the club's t-shirt. "How do you feel?"

"Better."

Bosco saw a delivery man walk into the bar. He winked at me then walked away.

"Here for something special?" Erika asked.

"A box of wings."

"That's all?" Her lower lip jutted out. It wasn't a good look. She was too old to pout.

"Did you talk to your brother?" I pointed at the side of my head.

She pulled her lip back. "I did."

"And?"

"He wasn't happy."

"And I'm not happy about the stitches. What about Croy?"

"I told him that the farm boy better keep his eyes open for you."

"Your brother would do better with some new friends."

She shrugged. "My parents were happy when he started hanging out with guys on the team."

"Nice. Did you tell them about the trouble this weekend?"

Erika shook her head. "Isaiah has had enough trouble with my parents. I don't need to add to it when things are finally leveling out." She motioned toward the kitchen. "I'll get the guys started on those wings."

She headed toward the back.

I wandered over to the bar where Max, the spiky-haired bartender, seemed to be taking inventory of the liquor bottles. "What's cooking, J.C.?"

"Wings."

"I don't understand how you like those things."

"There's no accounting for my taste, but I like your blue hair."

"For real?" He lightly rubbed his hand back and forth over his head. "I'm not sure if I'm in love with it. I'll prolly change it again."

"How many colors has it been this year?"

"Not counting my original—three." He left to continue preparing the bar.

I quietly sat on the stool and watched the crew move about the club. Occasionally, I would notice Erika eyeing me. It seemed more than a casual interest, but that was probably my imagination. She was an attractive woman, and most guys fell over themselves to talk with her. She never gave any guys from the club the time of day, and I'd never seen nor heard of her dating anyone. I knew better than to have my ego dashed against the rocks of truth.

Besides, I had a comfortable relationship with Tanya Robertson. She came and went as she pleased. I rarely saw her on my terms. I had never even been to her house. We never went out in public. When it first started, I thought it was perfect. Now, it seemed less so.

But it wasn't love, and that was important.

Erika walked out of the kitchen. She held a Styrofoam container. "Here you go."

I eyed the box. "What's this?"

"Your hot wings, silly." She glanced uncomfortably around. "What does it look like?" She hooked my arm and escorted me to the sidewalk.

Outside, I cast her a sideways glance. "This." My finger tapped the phone number written on top of the box.

"You live in the Claremont, right?"

I cocked my head.

"Don't tell me if you don't want."

"Yeah."

"What apartment?"

"Six thirty-three."

"I'll come by after closing. Call if anything changes."

Without another word, she turned and went back into the bar. Like an idiot, I stood on the sidewalk with a box of hot wings, trying to understand why a woman like her would make an offer like that.

Chapter 10

Down the block, several patrol cars were parked along the back of the Claremont. I rerouted to the front. Rounding the corner, I paused. More units were there, including a couple of unmarked.

Law enforcement at the Claremont wasn't uncommon. Usually, the management handled the low-level stuff like noise complaints, but over a hundred units of people struggling to get by can make for some hard times. That's when the police show up.

Usually, though, there weren't so many.

Inside, an older patrol officer stood with his hands in his pockets near the elevator. His belly pushed against his dark uniform shirt, straining the buttons. He wasn't wearing a ballistic vest. Maybe it was due to comfort. Perhaps he'd outgrown his old one. He reeked of garlic.

I pushed the elevator's call button, and the system whirred to life. "A lot of units outside."

He grunted something incomprehensible and eyed the Styrofoam container in my hand.

"What's going on?"

"Search warrant."

I nodded, thought for a moment, then asked, "Which unit?" It seemed a harmless question and one he wouldn't give me much grief over.

He looked over my shoulder to the front door. "Somewhere on the sixth."

Was it the woman who had the big man banging on her door? Had he returned and harmed her in some way?

The elevator continued to whirr.

"What have they got you doing?" I asked.

"Animal control." The heavy cop wheezed a deep breath. "Waiting around like a friggin' idiot for those jagoffs."

After shuddering to a stop, the elevator's doors clanged open. I placed my hand on the rubber bumper to keep the doors from closing. "What do you want them for?"

The cop thumbed toward the sky. "There's an out-of-control German Shepherd up there. No one knows—"

I jumped into the elevator and hit the button for my floor.

"Hey!" the cop said as the doors slowly slid closed. "You know something about that dog?"

The doors shut and the elevator climbed upward. When it jerked to a stop and opened, I sprinted down the hallway.

A group of police officers stood in front of Peyton's apartment. There were several uniforms and a suit. Even from this distance, I assumed the well-dressed one as a detective. The cops turned toward me with anticipation, and I slowed. The uniforms groaned in unison.

From inside the apartment, Corporal's bark was loud and menacing.

"What's going on?" I asked.

One of the patrol officers waved me away. "Go on. Back to your apartment."

I continued walking toward them.

The cop who'd taken an interest in me now stepped forward. "Didn't you hear me? Take a hike."

Holding a container of hot wings now felt foolish for a variety of reasons. I wanted to drop them right there in the middle of the hallway. "That's my friend's place." With my free hand, I pointed to Peyton's unit, then mine. "I live there."

The detective stepped forward now. His dark suit seemed nicely cut, and his green tie was imprinted with little elephants. His salt and pepper hair was a little longer than the others but well styled. His eyes were intense, but he had the trustworthy face of a father. "Detective Ackerman," he said.

I shook his extended hand. "John Cutler."

Ackerman motioned toward Peyton's apartment. "So, you know…?"

"Peyton Meyers? Yeah. His dog is Corporal."

An officer cracked opened the door to Peyton's apartment partway and said, "Sit, Corporal, sit!"

The Shepherd lunged, and the cop slammed the door closed. "Shit!" he hollered.

The assembled cops chuckled and shook their heads ruefully.

"What's going on?" I asked.

Ackerman's tongue darted across his lower lip. "We're executing a search warrant."

Now, I wanted to throw the stupid hot wings down the hall. Instead, I lowered my head and took a deep breath. "Search warrants are done in two instances—proof of crime or victim of crime. Which is it?"

The detective cocked his head. "Mr. Meyers was found this afternoon in an alley over near First and Lincoln."

First and Lincoln, I thought. What the hell was over there? Then I remembered that Eight Ball Billiards was about a block away. Was he on the way there to play a game? On the way home?

The detective's eyes softened. "I'm sorry."

I leaned my shoulders against the wall. The other cops had stopped their chuckling. The hot wings felt like a brick in my hand now.

Ackerman asked, "Does Mr. Meyers have any family in town? The building's management doesn't have any record of it."

"Peyton doesn't have any family."

"In that case, would you be willing to identify him for us?"

I nodded woodenly. "How did he die?"

"He was assaulted. Mind if I get your particulars? Name, birthdate, that sort of thing?" Ackerman bent his head and wrote as I responded to a series of rapid-fire questions. When he finished, he looked up. "Do you know anyone who would want to hurt Peyton?"

I didn't even hesitate. "Yeah. Hell, yeah."

Ackerman glanced at the other cops. "Who?"

"Wayne Sadler."

"Who's that?"

I quickly recounted Peyton's story to him. The other officers moved closer as I spoke. When I finished, Ackerman said, "Did Peyton report that incident to the police?"

"He was going to."

"I didn't see anything pop up in the system when I ran his name."

"Maybe he waited to do it today."

"Why wouldn't he have called it in immediately? Get it on the record that this fugitive was running around?"

I stayed silent. I'd put it into Peyton's head to delay reporting the assault. That was from my experience with law enforcement but primarily based on my cynicism of the police. I had once been one of them, but a poor experience on the way out scarred the way I perceived the profession. So did my recent experience in Seattle. Peyton and I had several talks about it. What if he had valued my distrust the most and not reported it at all?

The detective looked down the hallway as a broad-shouldered woman walked toward us. She carried a large pole with a loop of rope at its end—animal control.

"Wait," I said to Ackerman. "Don't take the dog out like that."

Ackerman frowned and tucked his notebook into a jacket pocket. "We have to. It needs to be at a shelter."

"If no one takes him, he'll be put down. He's not trained like a normal dog. He's harmless if handled right."

"You know how to do that?" Ackerman asked.

I nodded, hoping Corporal would respond to the commands even if they didn't come from Peyton.

The animal control officer eyed the detective. "If he wants to take the dog, fine. Just so long as someone accepts responsibility. It's better for us if he does."

Ackerman motioned toward the door. "It's your funeral." He winced at the reference.

I handed him my keys and the hot wings. "Would you unlock my apartment and put that inside? I'll grab the dog and bring him over."

The cops almost fell over each other to give me room to get to Peyton's door. From inside the apartment, Corporal continued to bark. I opened the door slightly, and the dog lunged. As firmly as I could, I ordered, "Corporal, parade rest."

The dog immediately quieted and sat on his haunches.

"Good boy."

A surprised murmur swept through the assembled officers. I slipped into Peyton's apartment.

"Hey, buddy," I said to the dog. "Who's a good dog? Don't eat me now. I'm your friend. Remember?"

Corporal watched me as I found his leash on the kitchen counter. Once the lead was attached to his collar, I said, "Forward, march."

The dog stood next to my side, and we left Peyton's apartment. The officers watched in astonishment at the change in Corporal's demeanor. Once inside my apartment, I unleashed the dog and said, "At ease." The Shepherd moved about my apartment and sniffed his new surroundings.

I stepped out of the unit and closed the door behind me.

The other cops muttered their comments of appreciation.

"I'll be damned," Ackerman said. "Drill and ceremony."

Motioning toward my friend's apartment, I said, "Peyton was a retired Marine. He taught the dog to bark at normal commands like sit and heel. He wouldn't have attacked unless commanded, but that bark is a scary thing."

"Hell, yeah, it is," one cop said. "Almost pissed myself."

The others laughed. I guess they forgot why they were there.

Ackerman leaned in, and he whispered. "Inside your apartment. There's a gun on the counter. Is it legal?"

"It's registered, and I have a carry permit."

The detective straightened. "After we get done here, can you come down and identify Mr. Meyers?"

"Yeah."

It didn't take them long to search Peyton's apartment. It was a small unit, and the crime hadn't occurred there. I wouldn't have expected it to take long.

While the detective was gone, I filled a dish with water and put it on the kitchen floor. "Here you go. We'll figure out your food situation later."

Corporal didn't seem interested. The dog turned and wandered through the apartment. I followed him, unsure if he might have to go outside. I even asked him as much. But he returned to the living room and dropped to the floor.

Satisfied the dog wasn't going to make a mess, I stared at the closed door of my apartment for some time. When that didn't bring satisfaction, I paced back and forth. The dog watched me circling. There was no reason to get started on something, though. I was sure as soon as I did, the detective would come knocking.

After a time, I grew tired of waiting and grabbed my hot wings. I'd just sat on the couch when there was a knock on the door.

When I opened it, Ackerman asked, "Ready?"

"Gimme a second."

I put the hot wings in the refrigerator then said to Corporal, "I'll be back. Don't eat the couch."

He didn't seem to understand.

Back in the hallway, DO NOT CROSS—POLICE LINE tape crossed over Peyton's door. After locking my unit, I followed the detective to his patrol car. In contrast to Ackerman's impeccable appearance, the maroon-colored vehicle was covered in grime. Someone wrote 'Wash Me' on the edge of the trunk. The detective swiped his hand through the words as he walked around to the driver's side.

When we got inside, Ackerman fired up the motor. "It's a twenty-minute ride to the medical examiner's office. Why don't you tell me a story?"

"What do you want to hear?" I pulled the seat belt across my chest.

"How'd a former Seattle Police Officer end up in the Claremont?"

I lifted an eyebrow.

"Dispatch ran your name. There were some entries in there and I asked them to dig deeper. Led back to Seattle."

I rested against the headrest. "It's a long story."

"It's a long drive."

"You don't want to hear it."

"Let me be the judge."

Ackerman dropped the car into gear and pulled away from the curb.

Chapter 11

The county morgue was in the lower level of Holy Family Hospital, a tired building with a prison's aesthetic appeal. Fluorescent lights hummed loudly and bathed the small room in stark white. Air conditioning kept the temperature at an uncomfortable level of cool while the aroma of bleach overwhelmed my sense of smell.

The medical assistant stood next to a sheet-covered body lying atop a stainless-steel gurney. He was a pale man with slightly bored eyes. When Detective Ackerman nodded, the assistant pulled the sheet back to reveal the head.

Even though the face was bloodied and mangled, there was no mistaking Peyton. He had been beaten to death—a terrible way to die. With how damaged his face was, it couldn't have been fast, and it must have been frightening. Maybe he blacked out early on. Strange to consider that, but I hoped that's what occurred.

I knew what would happen now. His body would remain in cold storage until an autopsy. A homicide investigation required one. Someone would cut Peyton open and remove his organs only to slice them into smaller bits. When everything was adequately sampled and labeled, the remaining pieces and parts would be tossed into a trash bag and tucked inside him. Then Peyton would be sewn up and sent out for cremation since there was no family to claim his remains.

I'd been to a couple of autopsies before. I didn't like the thought of my friend getting diced like an onion. That wasn't any worse than the reality on the steel gurney, though. For a moment, I wished I didn't have to be the one to identify him. It was a childish thing to think, though. He was dead, and this was the responsibility of the living.

Justice was also a responsibility of the living. Wayne Sadler, I thought. The man was walking around free while Peyton Meyers was about to get burned into nothingness. Soon, people wouldn't even remember him as a marine, father and husband, my friend. It would be as if he never existed. Maybe that's how we all end up.

"Well?" Ackerman asked.

"That's him."

The assistant medical examiner returned the sheet to its original position. Ackerman lightly grabbed my elbow and escorted me to the lobby.

"Someone beat him to death," the detective said. "Still think it was Sadler?"

"Who else?"

"Maybe it was random."

"Peyton wouldn't put himself into a situation where that could happen."

"People get into those situations whether they want it or not."

"Not Peyton. He was a Marine. His situational awareness was fine-tuned."

Ackerman jerked his head toward the exit. "Let's get out of here."

As we walked, I tried to hide my thoughts, but it must not have worked.

Once outside, Ackerman said, "Don't do it."

"Do what?"

"Interfere with an investigation. It's on your face." Ackerman dropped inside his car, and I followed suit.

"You're no longer a cop."

"No shit."

"And you're not a private investigator."

"Never said I was."

He pulled his seatbelt on. "So stop shining me on."

"How am I doing that?"

The car lurched forward when the detective popped it into gear. After we made the street, Ackerman glanced at me.

"You can't go poking around."

"Who said I was going to?"

He shook his head. "You know I do this for a living, right?"

"I know, and you're probably good at it."

"I meant dealing with people who lie. You're lying now about not getting involved."

I stared forward.

We traveled several blocks in silence until the detective said, "What happens if you scare the guy off?"

"He came back for revenge after Peyton beat him. Doesn't sound like he scares easily."

Ackerman eyed me. "Maybe he only hung around for that, and now he's left."

"Which takes him out of your jurisdiction."

"And means you'll be poking around for nothing. Don't waste your time."

"It's my time to waste."

Childish, I thought. Why was I acting this way?

I leaned my head against the passenger window and did my best to ignore Ackerman's continued warnings.

Chapter 12

Erika showed up shortly after midnight. I almost didn't register the timid knock, but the dog rustled and awoke me. Rubbing the sleep from my eyes, I opened the door. She still wore her Club Royale t-shirt.

"Did you forget?" she asked.

"Huh?"

"I said I would be by after work."

My hand ran over my head. "Oh, right." I thought about my stitches and brushed the hair in that direction.

She glanced back at the yellow police tape crossing over Peyton's front door. "What happened there?"

"My friend was murdered."

Erika unconsciously stepped backward and bumped into me. "Did it happen inside his apartment?"

"In an alley. Far from here." Ten blocks away wasn't far, but the fear in her eyes revealed she needed to believe it was as far away as possible.

"That's terrible."

"Yeah."

She looked into my apartment. "Are you going to invite me in?"

Cocking my head, I said, "This isn't a good idea."

"It's not?" She glanced back to Peyton's door. "Let me in, will ya? I'm getting weirded out."

I motioned her inside and closed the door behind her.

When Erika saw Corporal lying on the floor, she stopped and smiled. "You have a dog." She bent over and put her hands on her knees. "You never said you had a dog." She seemed genuinely happy to see him.

"He belonged to my friend."

She straightened, and her smile faded. She thumbed toward the hallway. "That friend?"

"Uh-huh." I turned on a table lamp, illuminating the room's corner and casting long shadows over the remaining walls.

Erika bent again and smiled at the dog. "What's his name?"

"Corporal."

"Like a soldier. Can I pet him?"

"He doesn't bother you?"

Erika dropped to a single knee. "Why would he do that?"

"Look at him. The first time I saw him, he scared the Jesus out of me."

She laughed. "Don't let my mother hear you say that. And it's bejesus."

"Bejesus," I muttered.

The dog's head lolled to the side as she scratched behind its ears. "Who's a good boy?" she cooed. Corporal's tail thumped on the floor.

"He likes you," I said.

Erika eyed me. "And I like you."

"C'mon." A smirk crossed my lips. "Don't."

"What?" She stood and moved toward me.

I stopped her by gently grabbing her arms. "Erika, let's not do this."

"Have I misread the way you watch me? It's been going on for months."

She tried to push forward, but I held her at bay.

"I don't think I can handle this," I said.

"You can't handle me?" She chuckled. "Whatever."

"Erika."

"Is it me, then? You don't find me attractive?"

"It's not that."

"Because I'm black?"

My face hardened, and she stopped pushing forward.

"Then what is it?"

"You're nice."

Now Erika's face flattened. She stepped back, and her arms slipped from my hands. "Nice? What the hell is nice? You don't want to be with me because I'm nice?" Her face pinched. "That may be the dumbest thing I've ever heard. Make up some better excuse than that. Nice."

She turned for the door.

I grabbed her hand. "Wait."

"Oh, now you want me to wait?" When she yanked her hand free, the dog raised its head. "Is this some game you play? Give a girl the eyes, and when she shows she's interested, you push her away."

"That's not it."

She thrust her finger at me. "Or maybe you think I do this all the time. Is that what you think? That I'm some kind of whore?"

"No, I—"

"That I hook up whenever I get the itch?" She pantomimed a little dance. "Well, I'll have you know, mister, that I haven't had a boyfriend in seven months. I haven't been with any man in that whole time either. I'm no whore. So, what made me think you were worth breaking the streak? I don't know. Maybe I thought you were nice." She extended her middle finger. "Well, fuck you, John."

I grabbed her hand again. "Please."

"What?" She didn't pull free.

"I'm sorry."

"You better be more than sorry."

"I'm not as nice as you think I am."

"Neither am I."

We watched each other for several moments. Finally, I said, "I am sorry."

Erika rolled her lips into her mouth as she thought. She stepped forward until we were chest to chest. "How sorry?"

Chapter 13

In the morning, Erika was gone. She was still in the air, though, and I smelled her on the pillow. With a push, I rolled out of bed, clicked off the alarm clock before it could sound, and made a pot of coffee.

Corporal got up from the floor and walked over. He seemed sad, so I patted his head. Was putting my emotions onto a dog stupid?

"I know," I said. "I'm sad, too." Was talking to it like a person also stupid?

The dog remained still under my hand. I tried not to take that as any sign other than he wanted some continued attention. We stayed that way for a couple of moments.

In the shower, the hot water scalded my body. I kept the stitches in my head from getting directly under the pelting water. Unfortunately, all the soap in the world wouldn't clean the image of Peyton on the gurney from my mind.

Afterward, I put on a pair of Levi's, my black boots, and a t-shirt. Corporal waited by the door. I commanded, "Parade rest," and clipped his leash on. At the door, I ordered, "Forward, march," and the dog fell in step. We headed to Riverfront Park. There weren't many people out at that time.

I learned drill and ceremony while in the police academy, so I understood the basic terms. One night over beers in his apartment, Peyton motioned toward Corporal. "He's a dog, but not a Devil Dog, so I had to dumb the whole thing down. I did the same thing for Private, too. The commands are mashed together into a single count instead of the traditional preparatory command followed by the order. Make sense?"

I said that it did, then Peyton ran down most of the phrases he'd already taught the dog.

At the park, I released the dog from his leash. "Fall out," I said.

Corporal took off with such a burst that I feared the dog might run out of the park. Instead, he was about fifty feet away when he banked hard and scampered around the area in a large loop. Whenever he slowed his gait, I whooped, which sent him into another bout of sprinting. I drank my coffee and watched the Shepherd sprint in large circles.

Ten minutes passed before the dog finally dropped to the ground. His tongue hung out of his mouth, and he panted loudly.

I pulled my cell phone from my pocket and made a call. The receptionist for the temporary labor service answered. After announcing the company name, she asked in a nasally tone, "How may we help you?"

"This is John Cutler. I can't take any jobs for the next couple days."

"Hold, please," she said, and the line went quiet.

Corporal rolled around in the grass, flipped upright, and darted off.

The receptionist came back on. "You have a job scheduled for tomorrow and Thursday."

"I can't do them. Personal reasons."

"But you're scheduled." The way she said it probably solved a lot of her problems.

"I won't be there." I snapped the phone closed.

The dog noticed the sharp noise. He stopped running and looked in my direction. His ears turned as if they were a pair of radar dishes.

"Come here," I called.

The dog remained where he was and continued observing the area.

"Devil dog," I muttered and finished the last of my coffee. "Fall in!"

The Shepherd sprinted over and stopped at attention. He stood with his back straight and his head held high. I clipped the leash on and ordered, "Forward, march."

On the walk back to the apartment, I thought about Peyton. I'm not sure if the dog thought about him, too, but I imagined it that way. It made me happy.

***

Back at the Claremont, I put Corporal in my apartment and walked over to Peyton's. The bright yellow police tape warned me to stay away. A little strip of tape was across the door and the jam. If anyone entered through there, the small strip would break, and the cops would know.

At the end of the hallway was the large window looking south. I pushed the pane up, climbed onto the fire escape, and closed it behind me. It was rarely open, so I didn't want to call attention to myself. I hadn't been out there before, but I immediately stepped over to Peyton's window. This wasn't a time to dawdle or screw around with sightseeing. I was outside the building on the sixth-floor fire escape. Anyone could see that I was about to attempt a felony.

Peyton's window was unlocked. Mine was often unlocked and opened because of the summer heat. It was a security issue due to the presence of the fire escape, but I only locked mine if I was going to be gone for an extended time. Other than that, what did I have that anyone would want to steal? Peyton probably felt the same way.

And Peyton usually had Corporal inside his unit. Securing it would be even less worrisome.

It took more effort than expected to open the window from the outside. Entering the apartment felt like disturbing the dead. The apartment was sweltering. I turned on an oscillating fan and pointed it toward the open window.

The first order of business was to collect Corporal's dog dishes and his food. I put the bowls into the large bag of food and carried it over to the window. I couldn't exit through the door because of the police tape.

Next, I set about finding anything Peyton might have kept about Wayne Sadler. It stood to reason that if Peyton thought daily about the man since his family's death, he must have saved something about him. At least, that's how I thought my friend would act. It's how I would have.

I felt like a thief for burglarizing Peyton's apartment but ransacking for mementos made me feel like a voyeur. I didn't like it.

On top of a kitchen cabinet was a shoebox. Inside were newspaper clippings of the accident that killed Peyton's family, Wayne Sadler's arrest, and subsequent fleeing. There was a folded copy of the original police report and court documents. A wanted flyer for Sadler was also there. There were two pictures of Wayne Sadler on the document. Neither was a booking photo, probably due to the broken nose he sustained during the crash. The first picture was of a smiling, fresh-faced kid. His eyes were bright, and his sandy-blond hair was collar length. The second photo of Sadler was a more somber piece. His eyes were still bright, but the hair was cut shorter, and he wore a dark-colored suit. The second photo seemed to be from an early court appearance, likely the bond hearing.

The man's physicals were laid out on the flyer. Six foot one. Hundred ninety pounds. Blond hair. Blue eyes. Tattoo of a rose on his left arm—no recorded scars.

I folded the flyer and put it back in the box. At the bottom of the container was a videocassette labeled with black marker—AMW.

Holding the tape, I glanced around the small living room then checked the bedroom. Like me, Peyton didn't have a television, which meant he didn't need a VCR. I tossed the videocassette back in the shoebox and put it next to the bag of dog food.

For several more minutes, I searched the apartment but didn't find anything else.

I crawled back onto the fire escape, closed the window, and carried the items back to my apartment.

Chapter 14

The knock on the door caused me to jump slightly. It was not because it was loud or jarring, but because I was intently concentrating on Wayne Sadler's information.

From his position in the middle of the room, Corporal lifted his head and watched the door.

Another tap came, and I called, "Just a minute."

"Okay," a woman responded.

I considered the various newspaper articles and the wanted flyer spread about the coffee table. I'd committed a felony to get these items, so it was probably best if I didn't openly announce my crime. I loaded the papers into the shoe box, affixed the lid, and put it under the table.

Outside my unit was the woman from apartment 617. She was in her late thirties and on the unhealthy side of skinny. Her dark complexion and the shape of her face led me to believe she was Hispanic.

She wore a faded yellow sundress and leather sandals. Her dark hair was around her shoulders, but she had applied make-up to hide the bruising around her eye. She crossed her arms around her waist. "Is this a bad time?"

"No." I pushed the door wider. "It's fine."

She started in but froze when she saw Corporal. Concern flashed in her eyes.

"He won't hurt you."

She glanced at me, then back to Corporal.

"I promise."

"Okay," she slowly said, but her tone revealed it was anything but. The woman walked over to the couch and sat. Her eyes scanned my apartment the entire time—the way a child does, the way someone afraid might.

I leaned on the wall near the window and waited. She came here to talk. There was no sense in rushing her.

Corporal flopped to his side and groaned. He was already bored with the new visitor.

"I'm sorry about your friend," the woman said. "The one who owned the dog." Her eyes drifted around my apartment some more. When they returned to me, she said, "I heard you used to be a cop."

"Where'd you hear that?"

"People talk. Is it true?"

"A lifetime ago."

Her gaze fell to her hands, which were now in her lap. "Why don't you do that anymore?"

"Things happen."

"They do, don't they?" she muttered. When she broke her trance, she looked up and said, "I'm Rosa."

"John."

"I want to hire you."

I frowned. "What for?"

"Protection."

"I don't do that."

Her eyes hardened—challenging now. "Why not?"

"I don't know. I guess I've never been asked."

"I'm asking."

I puffed my cheeks as I exhaled, thinking of a polite way to decline.

"I'll pay," she said. "I have money. Seven hundred dollars. It took a while to save, but I'll give it to you. All of it. For protection."

An additional seven hundred dollars sounded great, but I hadn't forgotten the size of her boyfriend, and Peyton wouldn't be there for backup. "I'm not your man."

Rosa averted her gaze, and red blossomed on her cheeks. She absently picked at the seam of her dress. "He rapes me when he's mad."

"Do you call the police?"

She shrugged. "Nothing ever happens." Tears welled in her eyes. "He only gets madder."

I scooted to the edge of my chair and leaned forward. "How come you haven't broken up with him?"

"I've tried." Rosa angrily brushed away the tears. "He doesn't agree."

"Maybe something will happen this time."

"He's already out." She pushed the hair from her face. "This is always the way. He gets in trouble and calms down. Then he says he's sorry and promises never to do it again. Until the next time." Her finger made several circles in the air. "Round and round." Her voice caught on the last word, and she inhaled in a stuttering fashion.

Grabbing the Marlboro soft pack from the coffee table, I extended it to her. After lighting both of our cigarettes, we smoked and listened to the fan whir.

As she calmed, Rosa watched the dog with an increasing fascination. "He's snoring."

"Like a semi stuck in low gear."

"Has he ever bitten anyone?"

"Not since he's been with me."

"You're not scared?"

"I'm scared of plenty, but not of the dog."

She cast a sideways glance. "Is that why you don't want to help? You're scared."

"He's a big man, Rosa. An angry man."

Her hand shook as she held the cigarette to her lips.

"His name is Houston, right?"

"Like the city. Yes."

"If he bothers you again, you can come down here."

She cocked her head. "But you said—"

"I don't do protection, but maybe I can help."

"I don't understand."

Neither did I, but I couldn't go into all the things I felt at that moment. Sure, I felt bad for her, but I didn't want to get mixed up with the big man again. The thought about discretion being the better part of valor lingered in my mind. I got away with fighting him the first time because Peyton was around. The second time might not go as well.

Was I afraid? Maybe. Was I hesitant? Hell, yes.

Rosa crushed her cigarette in the ashtray and stood. "So, if I need help—"

"You know where I live."

I followed her to the door and closed it after she left.

Chapter 15

When I hit the street with Wayne Sadler's wanted flyer folded in my back pocket, it was noon.

Eight Ball Billiards sat ten blocks east in the rapidly developing arts and entertainment district. A dinner theater, a jazz club, a concert house, and several trendy restaurants had popped up in the area over the past year.

Crack dealers and other street criminals had once overrun the neighborhood. That was before my time in the city. Now, it seemed most of that activity had been pushed into the alleys, the occasional abandoned building, or a genuinely rundown joint like the Hope Apartments.

The pool hall appeared to be a throwback to that rougher time. It didn't have the glitz or shine of the new establishments. In the windows were neon signs for brands like Pabst, Miller, and Captain Morgan. The inside seemed underlit except for the lights dangling over the pool tables. The resulting shadows provided a clandestine atmosphere.

The Allman Brothers Band's "Whipping Post" drifted lazily through the bar. My mother and her friends listened to that kind of music when I was growing up, so I was familiar with the song. It was about a man who remained with an unfaithful woman. Had I heard the song years ago, I might have identified what the singer felt and called it love. Now, I knew what it was and called it by its real name—addiction.

At the bar, I ordered a beer. The petite bartender didn't bother to ask for a preferred brand. She simply turned to the draft handle.

"Do you know Deacon?" I asked.

She glanced over her shoulder as the beer flowed but didn't say anything.

"Deacon," I repeated.

Pointing into a shadowy corner, she said, "The big guy."

I paid for the beer, grabbed my glass, and walked over to the pool tables. All were occupied with players, except the furthest one remained open. It had the newest felt, and its hanging lamp seemed the brightest. None of the waiting players even looked to that table. There must have been an off-limits sign somewhere that I couldn't locate.

Deacon sat alone on a bench that ran the length of the wall. Sweat beaded on his forehead. Red suspenders held up gray polyester slacks. His triple-extra-large, purple t-shirt claimed *Property of the University of Washington Athletic Department*. He must've tipped the scales at three-hundred fifty pounds.

"Table's taken," he said in a husky voice. He didn't make eye contact. Instead, he watched a game at another table.

"I'm not looking to play."

"Everyone plays." He reached over and grabbed a pool cue. Still not looking at me, Deacon appeared to be a fat king, surveying the billiard kingdom he lorded over. He tapped the cue three times on the hardwood floor. "Just depends on the game."

"I'm a friend of Peyton."

His gaze shifted. While his appearance might have been dumpy, there was something with the eyes. Something sharp. Something predatory. It felt as if he was sizing me up. The cue tapped once. "Where's Peyton?"

Motioning to the bench, I asked, "May I sit?"

"No. Where's Peyton?"

"He's dead."

Deacon cocked his head, which produced a fat roll on his neck and face. His eyes narrowed. "That so?"

I nodded.

"How?"

"Murdered. Yesterday, in an alley not too far from here."

"And you're his friend?"

"I am. John Cutler. Maybe he mentioned me?"

"He didn't." Deacon wiped his brow then dragged his hand across his t-shirt. "Cutler. Cutlery. In the cut," he muttered. It was probably a name remembering device he had. When he looked up, he asked, "How did you find out about this?"

"The cops came to his apartment and—"

"No," he interrupted. "This." He banged the pool cue twice on the floor. "Here."

I looked back and noticed two men in their mid-twenties moving closer to us. One black and one white, both in good shape. Neither held pool cues. Their movements weren't fast. They were trying to be subtle, but their eyes remained on me. Smaller, faster predators.

Turning to face Deacon, I said, "Peyton played with you. He invited me to come down a couple times."

Deacon studied me for a second more and tapped the cue once on the hardwood. His gaze returned to the other table.

Glancing over my shoulder, the two men drifted back into the shadows. With my attention back on Deacon, I'm sure my face revealed my irritation. I wanted to ask some simple questions and the fat man made his cronies known. It seemed he valued whatever power play this was more than helping a dead friend.

"You're the ex-cop?" Deacon asked.

"That's right."

"He asked if he could bring a friend who was an ex-cop. Never mentioned him by name. Now, you're here."

"I didn't know permission was needed."

He tilted his cue forward. "Play with the citizens any time you want, but not on this table."

"You're that good?"

"Good's got nothing to do with it."

"What's it got to do with?"

Deacon dismissively waved a thick finger. "Not a question you get to ask."

My hands balled, and the fat man's eyes flicked to them. His hand gripped the cue tighter. I forced myself to remain calm and extended my fingers. Deacon's attention remained on my hands, though.

"How'd you and Peyton meet?"

Now, he looked toward the front of the pool hall. Deacon waggled the cue back and forth, then side to side. I wondered if that was some sort of signal to the two guys. "Peyton was a good guy."

"He was."

"Served his country."

"Uh-huh."

"I like people who serve others." He glanced at me. "The world needs more like that. Like what the bible says."

"Is that what you do?"

His eyes slanted. "You keep stepping on yourself. I would have expected better."

"I'm trying to find who did this to Peyton. Since he was your friend, maybe you might want to help."

Deacon turned away. He waggled the cue again. "Do

the cops have any suspects?"

I pulled out the wanted flyer from my back pocket, unfolded it, and extended my hand. "Ever seen this guy?"

Deacon made no motion to take the paper from me. "I don't think so."

"Would you tell me if you did?"

The heavyset man eyed me. "You're an abrasive man, Cutler."

"I get that way when my friends are murdered." I flicked the wanted flyer. "I think this guy is responsible. That's an old picture. Fifteen years or so. Take another look. Please."

Deacon looked briefly away before deciding something. Then he leaned slightly toward me but never touched the paper. "Maybe he looks familiar. I don't know. But there was a guy in here yesterday with a rose tattooed on his left arm, just like it says there. I can't say it's the same guy as the one in this picture, but this guy's face was banged up. Came in with a real mean on—if you get my drift. Just walked through the joint like he was looking for trouble."

"You're sure?"

"Am I sure some the guy wanted trouble? Yeah, Cutler. I know an asshole when I see one." He cocked his head. It wasn't hard to get the meaning behind that statement. "Am I sure that particular asshole was this guy?" He tapped the flyer. "Not at all. I'm going off the fact the guy had a rose tattoo and a busted-up mug. Neither is uncommon in these parts." He motioned to my stitches. "Looks like someone left you a calling card."

Ignoring his slight, I asked, "Did this guy say anything when he was here?"

"Didn't have to. He had on a Playground tank top. That

told me everything I needed to know."

"Playground?"

Deacon frowned. "The Playground is a Dog Town dive. We beat them in last year's tournament."

"Where's Dog Town?"

"How long have you been in town? It's slang for Hillyard. I take it you know where that is?"

"Up north." Hillyard had a reputation for being the roughest section of Spokane. "How were you so sure he wanted to start trouble?"

"He strolled through mean-mugging everyone. When he didn't find any takers, the guy just left. I thought nothing of it when it happened. He seemed one of those types itching for a fight. That happens now and then, but nobody ever really fights in here. This is a nice, friendly place."

The way he said it didn't make it seem so nice or friendly. I glanced back for the two men. They were somewhere in the shadows.

Turning back to him, I folded the flyer and slipped it into my back pocket. "Maybe this guy was out looking for Peyton."

"From what you said, it seems as if he may have found him."

***

After leaving Eight Ball Billiards, I crossed Monroe Street and headed into the nearest alley. According to Detective Ackerman, Peyton was found near First and Lincoln. That was only a block away. It either occurred in this stretch of alley or the next. I crossed the street and confirmed my suspicions.

Dried blood, a single rolled-up rubber glove, and a foot of crime scene tape were the lingering remains of a homicide investigation. This was where Peyton had died violently.

The sightline up and down the alley was good, but there wasn't much visibility from any other angle. The buildings that bracketed this stretch had windows on higher floors, but none at ground level. I understood why. I wouldn't want to watch a bum defecating, either.

And just because the upper floors had windows lining the alley didn't mean anything. The workers who had offices with windows would have had to see the beating take place, which meant being in the right place at the right time. An employee could have been in their office at the right time but not even faced toward their window. They might have missed Peyton's murder because they were doing something as mundane as deleting junk email.

Or worse, maybe an office worker witnessed the altercation but didn't do anything. What might it have looked like to them? How many quarrels between homeless men had I turned away from because I didn't want to be involved? When I was a cop, I had a duty to intervene. As private citizen John Cutler, I had no such obligation. Why would I assume others should?

An upper-floor employee might have simply turned away at the start of the altercation and not wanted to get involved. Or they might have continued to sip a cool beverage in an air-conditioned office while they watched Wayne Sadler beat Peyton Meyers to death. Then they turned around and returned to deleting junk email.

There were plenty of times in my life when I did something similar. But not this time. Peyton was my friend. I was pushing my chips into the middle of the table.

Still, whoever killed Peyton must have had something significant to lose if he was willing to risk the chance someone *might* have seen and then called the police. The safe money—my money now in the middle of the table—was on Wayne Sadler.

I spent a few more minutes in the alley, looking for anything that the cops might have overlooked—false hopes of finding a dropped driver's license or a pawn ticket danced in my head. I tried to convince myself that stranger things have happened. When the realization eventually hit home that the investigators missed nothing, I continued east to collect my truck.

My next stop was too far to walk.

Chapter 16

A block away from the Playground, I waited and watched.

The bar resided at the northeast corner of Market Street and Crown Avenue in a red concrete box. Banners hawking various beers were plastered along the sides of the building. One vinyl sign proudly announced it was "voted Spokane's diviest dive bar."

Dusty pick-ups, dented sedans, and a few work trucks filled the parking lot. There was even a rusting station wagon, a nearly extinct beast slain by the advent of the minivan. I couldn't remember the last time I'd seen one of those.

Customers wandered in and out of the establishment. Men and women. Young and old. Fat and thin. But there were two consistent themes to the patrons—economically depressed and white. The rest of the country might be experiencing financial growth, but the folks drinking at the Playground looked anything but prosperous.

And with the number of confederate flags on the vehicles in the parking lot, persons of color were encouraged to drink elsewhere.

My gun was in the glovebox. It was illegal in Washington State to bring a firearm into a liquor establishment, even with a carry permit. But only the lawful followed the laws, I reminded myself. There had to be a gun or two already inside the Playground.

Judged by twelve or carried by six, I thought. No. It was stupid to make decisions based on a hollow platitude. If there was trouble inside the bar, I'd be better off talking my way out of it than trying to bully my way with a gun. Besides, the weapon might give me a false sense of security, a feeling of toughness. It was better to be intelligent and respectful and retreat if need be. I was already thinking withdrawal, and I hadn't even gone inside.

Then get going, I scolded myself. Stop trying to find a reason not to go in.

Dropping my truck into gear, I pulled into the parking lot and stopped alongside a primer gray Chevy Nova with a rebel flag sticker in its back window. Inside the emblem were the words, 'If the south would've won, we would've had it made.'

An aroma of stale beer and cigarette smoke greeted me after I yanked open the bar's door.

Heads turned, and wary eyes watched me. It wasn't paranoia. I was an outsider. It didn't matter to them that I shared the same economic rung or that my skin color was the same. What mattered was my unfamiliar face, and that meant one thing in this bar—danger.

Maybe I was a narc looking for a bust.

Or a process server delivering divorce papers.

At best, I was just an asshole who stumbled into the wrong joint.

Whatever I was, they weren't going to make me feel welcome.

The stuttering bass line for Thin Lizzy's "Bad Reputation" pounded through two speakers suspended from the ceiling. This broke the new-guy trance, and the place erupted with activity.

A nearby table of men howled as the song started. One man moaned, "Not again," then laughed. Two women in their late forties danced and bounced at the jukebox while they selected songs.

"Bad Reputation" was an unmistakable tune. Another I knew because of my mother's friends. She would never listen to it now. Doing so wouldn't look right.

Watching these patrons nod so approvingly to the song, I thought about the confederate flags in the parking lot. They probably didn't know Thin Lizzy's lead singer was of mixed heritage. Or maybe they did, and it didn't bother them because of how good the song was. I doubted that, though. They didn't seem the forgiving type.

The bartender was rail thin with distrusting eyes. He stood about my height but probably weighed in at less than a hundred sixty pounds. His skin was dingy gray, and his long, stringy hair receded from the temples. He wore a faded blue workman's shirt with a dark patch over his left breast where a nametag had once been. "What'll you have?"

"Beer." I surveyed the bar in the mirror, looking for Wayne Sadler. He wasn't there. Maybe he was in the restroom.

The bartender returned with a beer and placed it on the bar. "Three-fifty." We exchanged money, and he walked to the opposite end of the bar. He leaned against the back counter and folded his arms over his chest. He was doing his best to appear disconnected.

The jukebox pounded one song after another, each one eliciting whoops and groans from various tables. The Steve Miller Band sang "Take the Money and Run," then Molly Hatchet belted out "Flirtin' with Disaster." The patrons seemed to enjoy the tunes, and someone occasionally hollered out a comment supporting its choice. Somewhere after Hatchet, I lost interest in the music. The songs became ones I couldn't identify or had never heard of before. Well, one sounded sort of familiar, but who the band was, I had no idea, and I couldn't place where I might have heard it.

After a time, the bartender came over. "Another?"

I nodded, and he refilled my warm glass. Wordlessly, we exchanged money, and he returned to his perch at the end of the bar.

Whenever the bar door swung open, sunlight washed in. Before long, only darkness greeted each opening.

More songs played. People came and went. Wayne Sadler never came out of the restroom or through the front door.

About an hour later, the bartender came back over. "Done nursing that one?"

"I'll take another."

The bartender took the glass, poured out the dregs that remained, and went to refill it. I'd spent enough time hoping. It was time to act. While the bartender was at the draft handles, I pulled the wanted flyer from my back pocket and unfolded it. I laid it on the counter and put a twenty on top of it.

When the bartender returned with my beer, I said, "Keep the change."

He eyed the bill suspiciously before slowly picking it up. His gaze remained on Wayne Sadler's picture. He leaned over the document and appeared to read it.

"Ever see that guy?"

The bartender's gaze shifted to me. Then he rolled his eyes and moved toward the end of the bar.

I returned the flyer to my pocket and scanned the crowd in the back bar mirror. A few patrons watched me intently. Coming to the Playground was my master plan for finding

Wayne Sadler, but maybe it was time to leave. There was nothing wrong with retreating and coming back another day. And wasn't this why I'd left my gun in the truck? So I wouldn't be tempted to do something foolish?

Foghat's "Slow Ride" started on the jukebox, and the tenor of the crowd changed. Smiles erupted on most of their faces, and several of them clapped.

Movement at the end of the bar caught my eye. The bartender was now on the phone with his back to me.

Several of the patrons shouted along with the chorus. "Slow ride!"

The two women were back at the jukebox, jumping and bouncing again.

Hunched over with one hand covering his bare ear, the bartender shouted into the phone. He nodded, yelled something again, and hung up. When he turned around, he noticed me. His lip curled, and he averted his gaze.

As most of the customers enjoyed Foghat's anthem to sex, the whole bar seemed to enter a party zone. The next song amped them up higher. Bachman-Turner Overdrive's "Takin' Care of Business" got several tables of customers standing and spinning with joy. Soon, the whole bar stomped their feet to the pounding tune.

"Takin' care of business!" some customers yelled.

Others hollered back, "Every day!"

When that tune ended, Grand Funk Railroad's "We're an American Band" threatened to blow the roof off the place. Instead of watching their reflection in the mirror, I spun around and watched the crowd now. Everyone was up from their tables. It was a sight. The whole place was laughing and singing along with the jukebox. The two women who had started the playlist hopped around holding hands and high-fived any takers. They even bounced by me and slapped my outstretched palm.

When that song ended, nothing followed. Silence descended over the Playground. It was like the air was sucked out of the joint. A collective groan erupted. The two women collapsed into their chairs. Several people rushed for the jukebox. I turned back to the bar.

The bartender walked over and pulled my beer away. "Shove off."

"I'm not done."

"Yeah, you are." He looked around the now quiet bar then loudly pronounced, "We don't serve cops."

"I'm not a cop."

"We don't serve bounty hunters, either." Another loud declaration.

My gaze flicked toward the mirror. The patrons viewed me with collective distrust. The folks at the jukebox even watched. There would be no music coming to my rescue.

The bartender strutted toward the opposite end of the bar, swinging his arms as he went. He turned, flicked his stringy hair from his shoulders, and stuck a straw in his mouth.

There was no need to stay any longer.

***

Outside the bar, it was dark. The night sky was clear, but the streetlights blocked any stars from being seen. At my truck, I dug into my pocket for my keys.

Shuffling footsteps caused me to turn. Three rejects from a 1980s heavy metal video hurriedly approached. None of them were Sadler, and none of them had been inside the bar, but they all looked pissed. I left my keys in my pocket and pulled my hand out. There was no way I could make it inside the truck before they would be on me. I put my back against my rig.

Each of the men wore blue jeans, dirty white high-tops, and black concert t-shirts.

The Van Halen fan with a thin smile asked, "We hear you're lookin' for someone." When he spoke, only a single tooth was visible in the upper front of his mouth.

"Not me," I said.

A twitchy guy in a Metallica shirt moved to my left. This one's eyes were too close together, and his mouth hung open. On my right was a guy in a Mötley Crüe shirt with droopy eyes and an ugly scar across his nose.

The three men triangulated me without much effort.

"That's not what we heard," One Tooth said.

"What did you hear?"

Twitchy pointed. "You're looking for Mitch."

One Tooth swung a backhand at Twitchy. The smaller man ducked even though he was out of the other's range.

"What I do?" Twitchy whined.

"You said his name," One Tooth said.

Twitchy scowled at me as the left side of his face spasmed.

Wayne must have changed his name. It made sense. The man couldn't have hidden all these years under the identity of Wayne Sadler.

"Where can I find Mitch?" I asked.

One Tooth stared at Twitchy. "You see?"

"It was an accident."

"It's always an accident with you, same as with your mother."

Twitchy waved at me. "But he was looking for him. He knew his name."

One Tooth shook his head. "Cliff said he had a different name."

The bartender was Cliff, and he'd called these guys to put a scare into me. Why?

"We need to focus," Scarface said.

He was right. I did need to focus. Waiting for the three of them to stop bickering and devise a plan was asking for trouble. I needed to act first.

One Tooth was the closest. That made him the unlucky one. I snapped a jab into his nose.

Twitchy grunted, "Nuh!" in surprise, and Scarface shouted, "Hey!"

One Tooth brought his hands up to cover his nose. He shouldn't have done that. My follow-up punch—a right cross—hit him in the back of his hands. One Tooth squealed and backpedaled several steps. This movement created a break in their containment.

I sprinted north.

"He's running!" Twitchy shouted.

My boots slapped the concrete as I raced northbound along Market Street. It didn't take long for my lungs to burn. I glanced over my shoulder and saw two of them in pursuit. Scarface was almost a block back, but Twitchy kept running stride for stride with me within a few feet.

In the middle of the next street, I stopped and spun. Twitchy leaped from the curb before my turn and couldn't slow his momentum now that he was airborne. When he landed, he took two stuttering steps before I kicked him. He tried to protect himself by hopping a little and shoving his hands toward my leg. All that did was marry gravity to my strike.

The toe of my boot hit his testicles as his hands touched my shins. Twitchy emitted a squeaky scream before crumpling to the ground in a twisting, rolling motion.

Half a block away, Scarface halted—perhaps surprised at my attack on his partner. He yelled something incoherent, and then he bolted toward me with renewed vigor.

I cut through an alley in the direction of Haven Street. When I exited, I turned south to head back toward my truck. My heavy footsteps blocked the sounds of a possible pursuer. I stole frequent glances over my shoulder and realized that Scarface had given up the chase. Maybe he has stayed with his friend.

When I arrived at Crown Street, I slowed. In the distance, One Tooth was hunched over. He held onto the back of my truck as he spat and swore. People walked by on their way into the Playground. A man asked something, and One Tooth let loose a string of expletives.

My lungs ached, and my legs felt like sandbags, but I pushed forward as quickly and quietly as possible. As I neared the Playground, the music from the bar covered my movements. At the last moment, One Tooth turned toward me. Blood covered his lips and chin.

"The fuck?" he gasped just before I punched him again.

He staggered backward and fell. Landing on his side, he held out his hand in weak defense. I smacked it away.

"Where's Wayne?"

"Who?"

"Mitch." I kicked him in the shin, and he squealed. My boots were not forgiving.

"Where's Mitch?" I asked.

"I don't know! I don't know!"

"How do you know him?"

One Tooth shook his head. He raised his hand again. Another weak defense that I turned to my advantage. I grabbed his fingers and twisted them.

In more pain now, One Tooth hollered, "He's my partner."

"Doing what?"

I twisted his fingers further.

"We deal. We deal!"

"Dope?"

"Bud! Let go!"

"Hey," a man yelled. An elderly couple stood near the bar's entrance. "Get away from him."

I ignored the couple and focused on One Tooth. "How do I find Mitch?"

"We're calling the cops!" the older man yelled. The couple hurried inside.

"Get away from him," someone else yelled from down the street. Scarface and Twitchy were almost back to the bar.

Was I afraid of the cops? No. But if the older man brought patrons back outside, the odds would not be in my favor. Or if Scarface and Twitchy made it to me, then they weren't going to fall for any surprises this time.

The door of the bar opened, and several customers stumbled out. "There!" the older man hollered. "Over there."

I let go of One Tooth's hand and ran to my truck. I pulled out my keys and climbed in. More people exited the Playground.

The truck reversed several feet, and I hoped I wouldn't run over One Tooth. There wasn't a bump. I dropped it into gear and sped out of the parking lot. Twitchy and Scarface threw rocks at me as I went by.

My heart pounded as I raced through residential neighborhoods. Once I made it to Crestline Street, I turned south and drove until I pulled into the lot of a defunct mechanic's shop.

Breathing deep, I tried to calm myself. My hands shook, my mouth was dry, and my stomach turned. It was the adrenaline, and I was coming down. I'd come close to a beating, maybe worse.

I was playing detective and needed to be smarter. Wayne Sadler was wanted for fleeing justice. He was running drugs. He had friends who were willing to rough me up for snooping around.

I didn't have any backup or a badge. The only thing I had was my wits. It was time I started acting like I had some.

***

I drove side streets for some time before heading home. Wayne Sadler had to be spooked now. There was no other way to wrap my head around it.

First, Peyton attacked him in an alley. Then he returned downtown looking for retribution—Deacon confirmed that. Unless he was a stone-hearted killer, Wayne had to be worried that someone saw him murder Peyton. Then I showed up at the Playground asking about him. The guy would be in the wind now.

Club Royale's parking lot was half full. Music pounded from inside the bar. Tuesday nights were terrible for the club, almost as bad as Mondays, but Bosco kept it open. Not that I cared, because all I wanted at that moment was a place to hide my truck. I worried that One Tooth and his friends might have found a way to follow me. I locked my pickup and activated the alarm.

Walking back to the Claremont, I mentally criticized

myself. From leaving my gun in the truck to announcing that I was searching for Wayne Sadler, the night was a monumental screw-up that I wanted to forget.

But I had learned two important things. First, Sadler was dealing drugs. Second, he was living under an assumed name—Mitch something or other.

After unlocking my apartment, I stepped in long enough to leash Corporal. We walked over to Riverfront Park in the heavy August heat. The lights of downtown made the night a dark gray. An almost full moon hung in the sky.

The dog sprinted in circles before locating a spot to drop a present for the grounds crew. I should have picked up his mess, but I reasoned that I'd forgotten to bring a poop bag. Of course, I hadn't forgotten, but I promised myself to remember next time.

For a moment, Corporal disappeared into the dark. A wave of loneliness was followed by a panic that he might have run away. "Fall in," I hollered. My voice boomed through the park.

The dog burst through the bushes and sprinted toward me. He stopped with his tongue drooping out.

I put his leash on. "Let's get you home."

"Hey, man," a scratchy voice called out.

A dirty man in camouflaged pants and a dark t-shirt approached. He carried a large stick in his hand and walked with an unsteady gait. "Gimme some money."

"No."

"Gimme money!"

My hand tightened around Corporal's leash. "Present arms."

The German Shepherd bared his teeth and growled.

The man stepped forward and raised the stick above his

head. "Fuck that dog!"

"Fire," I shouted.

The dog jumped forward and tugged at his leash. He barked wildly, and it took two hands to hold him back.

"Shit!" the man screamed. He stumbled off into the trees.

"At ease," I commanded.

Corporal dropped to the ground.

We watched and listened. A minute passed before I decided it was safe to move. We marched back to our apartment along the well-lit streets. When we stopped at a crosswalk, I reached down and stroked the dog's head.

"You're a fine trooper."

Thoroughly unimpressed by the night's confrontation, Corporal lifted his leg and pissed on a lamp post.

Chapter 17

In the morning, I drank a cup of coffee while reading a dogeared copy of Raymond Chandler's *The Big Sleep* that I found a week ago in the Claremont's dayroom. I wasn't much of a reader, but I wanted to be. If I finished this book, it would be my fourth for the year. It was taking me about two months to finish a book. Not great production by any stretch of the imagination, but at least I tried.

The problem with reading this morning was my focus kept wandering to Peyton's murder and the confrontation I had the previous evening at the Playground. I thought about calling Detective Ackerman and telling him what I discovered. The lead on Wayne Sadler hanging out at the Playground was a viable one, but I hadn't done anything except get in a fight and let the man know someone was after him.

If I called Ackerman, there was one thing that he would surely tell me to do—stay out of it. I didn't want to do that.

My brow furrowed as my eyes scanned the page I was on. I'd lost my place. Hell, I couldn't even remember what I'd just read. A knock on the door saved me from a futile search. Corporal perked up from where he napped. Slapping the paperback closed, I tossed it onto the coffee table.

Rosa stood in the hallway and held a plate covered by aluminum foil. She wore a pair of frayed denim shorts and an oversized white t-shirt with a droopy collar. "Have you eaten breakfast?"

"No."

She extended the dish. "Here you go."

When I accepted the warm plate, she self-consciously crossed her arms. I motioned toward the kitchen with my head. "Want to come in?"

Rosa followed me into the apartment and closed the door behind her.

I put the dish on the kitchen table. "I don't have cream for the coffee, but you're welcome to some."

"That's fine."

I filled a mug, and we sat at the table. Carefully, I peeled back the aluminum foil and exposed two warm burritos.

Rosa leaned forward, and pride filled her eyes as she examined her handiwork. "They have eggs, onions, potatoes, and sausage in them. Oh, and chipotle." She looked up. "Is spicy okay?"

"It's great. Do you want one?"

"I already ate. I had too many potatoes and sausage, so I made these for you. If you don't like them, give them to the dog."

"Are you kidding? They look fantastic."

The flavor exploded in my mouth, and I wolfed the first one down. It was almost embarrassing to eat that way in front of her. *Almost.* I pushed the plate to the side and saved the second burrito. "For later," I said.

That seemed to make her happy.

"Thank you."

She lifted her cup. "You're welcome."

I pulled my coffee to me. "What's the latest on your boyfriend?"

She shrugged. "The judge gave him a No Contact Order."

"That's standard in domestic violence cases. He can't even call you now without getting arrested."

"We'll see." She didn't sound convinced of the system's effectiveness.

From the coffee table, I retrieved my cigarettes and the ashtray. I offered her one, and she accepted.

I asked, "What do you do for a living?"

"Nothing right now."

Sadness crossed her face, and it seemed she wanted to say more. I waited for her to continue.

"A couple years ago, I broke down." The words hung in the air for a heartbeat. Then she tapped her head with the fingers holding her cigarette. "Everything folded in on itself. I wasn't—" She inhaled on the cigarette then held the smoke. When she exhaled, her tongue darted over her upper lip. "I was married before. We were both out of work and needed money for rent and food. We were behind on our utilities. Neither of us had family to turn to. Didn't have any state help either." She nodded a few times. "Things were looking up, though. I got hired for a good job. I was to be a secretary for one of those armored transport companies—the ones that deliver money for businesses and banks. Do you know what I'm talking about?"

"Yeah."

"But the job didn't start for two weeks, and we were still hurting for money. They don't pay you *until* after you put in some hours. Funny how that works." She flicked her cigarette's ash into the little tray. "My husband got the bright idea to rob a flower shop. He walked right in, stuck his finger in his jacket, and held them up."

I tapped my cigarette over the tray. "I'm not advocating robbery, but there's gotta be a hundred better places to rob than a flower shop."

"I wish you would have talked with him before. Hell, I

wish he would have talked with me before. No. He just went and did it. After he was arrested, he said he was tired of me always taking care of our problems. He wanted to be the one for once."

"And robbing a flower shop was the answer?"

"He didn't think the ladies who worked there would put up a fuss. He didn't have a gun—just his thumb and finger." She mimed the action with her hand. "And it was Valentine's Day. He thought the store would have all sorts of cash from rich guys getting flowers for their wives." Her laugh was hollow. "That's where he made his mistake."

"Not his only one."

She canted her head toward me. "He thought it would be cash-heavy because of the holiday. All we ever scraped together was cash, but rich people don't use cash. They use credit cards."

My previous life's credit card was now maxed out, making it worthless as anything except a minimum payment albatross.

"For thirty-seven dollars and a dozen roses, he was sentenced to two years. It was the first time he ever brought me flowers. The cops took them for evidence, though. I got to keep them for about two hours." She sighed. "They were pretty."

"Seems like he got off light for a robbery."

"I guess. He had never done anything like that before, and his attorney got him a plea deal." She sipped her coffee. "Anyway, the good job I had been hired for? Poof. Gone. They said they had legitimate security concerns since my husband was arrested for robbery. I tried to tell them he did that on his own—that I didn't know anything about it. And I didn't, I swear to God." She crossed herself like they do at church. "But they didn't care. The risk was too great, they said. Moral turpitude. Have you ever heard such a word? Turpitude? I hadn't, but that's why they fired me. Before I ever started. I went home that day and saw a red notice on our house. The city shut off our water. I don't normally swear, but I did that day—a lot. I went to the nearest convenience store, bought the only bottle of wine I could afford, and blasted myself into orbit. After that, I melted down."

She ground out her cigarette. "A doctor said I was depressed. He prescribed me some meds. They made me feel worse. Now, I guess I've gotten used to them." She stared at the ashtray for a few moments. Embarrassment slowly washed over her face. "I'm sorry."

"For what?"

"Dumping my story on you. I shouldn't have done that." She stood. "Bring the plate back when you're done with it." She moved toward the door.

"Hey."

Rosa stopped with her hand on the knob.

"Do you have a VCR?"

"Huh?"

I walked over to the coffee table and pulled the shoebox out from under it. I removed the videotape and held it up. "I found this in Peyton's apartment."

"Is it a movie?"

"I don't know what it is."

She opened the door. "I have a VCR."

***

Rosa's apartment was nicer than mine. The living room had the same couch and chair that I did since the apartments came furnished, but her stuff looked newer.

She had also dressed up her furniture with a brown and tan afghan folded over the couch's back, and small arm-covers rested in the appropriate places on the chair. The door to her bedroom was closed.

She held her hand out for the videotape.

An aroma of vanilla hung in the apartment. I also caught a whiff of cleaning products. I wondered if Rosa even smoked in her apartment.

On a stand in the corner was an older, boxy television set. Next to it sat a plant in a ceramic pot. Underneath on a lower shelf was a VCR. Rosa pushed the tape into the VCR, turned on the television, and handed me the remote control. I sat on the couch and started the video.

There was the usual static before a picture came into focus. It was a commercial, based upon the cheesiness of the clothing and music. A balding white man in his sixties rapped about lending money for car purchases with no credit required. Two black teenagers stood next to him. The kids wore brightly colored leather jackets and flip-up sunglasses. Their haircuts were long on top but tight along the sides. The kids danced with smiles and animatedly clapped while the older man continued his capitalist rap.

I cringed at the image and glanced at Rosa. She shook her head.

After the commercial ended, a middle-aged white man in a brown leather jacket appeared. The man was immediately familiar, not only to a former cop but most television viewers. The host introduced that night's episode and provided a brief rundown of the upcoming segments. He talked about a child rapist who escaped from custody, a cop killer still at large for over six months, and a fugitive who fled before facing justice in a vehicular homicide case.

I sat upright, immediately understanding why Peyton kept the tape.

Rosa noticed my sudden interest. "Is everything okay?"

"Uh-huh."

When the first segment appeared, it was about a child rapist that fled from a Nashville jail. I forwarded through that portion. More commercials appeared, and I continued scanning beyond them. The show's logo flashed, and I returned the tape to normal speed. The host introduced a segment about a fugitive known as Wayne Sadler.

As the host narrated, pictures and video clips were shown. Several included Peyton's family as well as Sadler's. Footage from local television news programs was relied upon heavily.

When Peyton was interviewed, Rosa whispered, "That's your friend."

It was sad to see Peyton alive on the screen and know he was gone. Probably the same way he must have felt watching news archival footage of his daughter playing high school volleyball.

Because of the show, I got a good look at Sadler. In the pictures, he was in his late teens. Wayne Sadler's rose tattoo filled up the screen for several seconds while the host described his features.

When the segment ended, the television screen turned into a blizzard. I ejected the tape from the VCR.

"Did you find what you wanted?" Rosa brought her legs underneath her while still seated on the chair.

I gave her a quick recap of the conversation I had with Peyton before his murder. I even included the information I got from Deacon and my screw-up at the Playground. Rosa listened quietly.

"He's been on the run for fifteen years," I said, "and no

one's caught him yet. Then he bumps into Peyton, and my friend winds up murdered in an alley."

"Couldn't it be a coincidence? Couldn't someone else have murdered your friend?"

"Peyton was murdered because he found Wayne Sadler. The guy has been hiding all these years because of what he did. You saw it." I pointed at the darkened TV. "Sadler had to know Peyton wouldn't let it sit. He probably figured Peyton lived in the area, so he came back hunting for him. I saw how badly Peyton looked. His murder was revenge."

"Do you think this man is still in town?"

"I don't know."

She studied me. "What will you do if you find him?"

"I'm going to call the cops and let them take him."

"You're not seeking vengeance?"

"Vengeance is for the movies."

Rosa seemed confused. "If that's not what you want, then let the cops find him."

"It's been fifteen years, and they haven't yet. Listen, here's the difference. For the cops, it's a job. I met the detective assigned to this case, and he seems like a decent guy, but he's only working on Peyton's murder until it's time to go home. Let's say he's working a nine-hour day. During that time, he's got to balance Peyton's case with all the other cases he's been assigned. God knows how many that could be. He's also got to fit the rest of life's drama in. Maybe a wife and some kids. Maybe an ex-wife and some other kids. I don't know. But what I do know is that Peyton isn't anything more than a name on a case file to this guy. For me, this is personal. It's the only priority I've got."

Rosa cocked her head. Her eyes questioned my tirade.

"What?" I asked.

"You used to be a cop."

"And?"

"You seem to hate them."

"I don't hate them." I stood. "But I hate who I became while I was one of them. That's a truth I will never escape."

Her eyes widened.

"I'm sorry," I said.

"For?"

I thought about her earlier words. "Dumping on you. I shouldn't have done that."

Her smile was soft and forgiving. "I guess we're even, then."

I popped the tape from the VCR and headed for the door. "Thank you for letting me watch this."

Chapter 18

After two, I headed to Club Royale. Even though Peyton's murder was a priority, I needed to keep the one job that was a consistent form of income. I could be flippant with the temporary gigs—there were plenty of those—but bouncing was a decent job for my skillset.

It was early, so only the staff were inside. Bosco was near the backroom, accepting an order from a distributor.

Max prepped for the upcoming night. He looked up from his notepad. I motioned toward his head. His formerly blue hair was now a garish orange. "Is there a name for that color?"

He frowned. "Ugly is what I call it."

"What the hell happened?"

Max ran his fingers through his hair and leaned on the counter. His tone became conspiratorial. "After work last night, some of us went back to my place. A few others showed up. You remember how things happened like that when you were young."

"Not really."

"That explains a lot." He rolled his eyes. "Anyway, we got drunk, smoked a little, and a couple guys who are into that *Queer Eye* show wanted to make me over. Have you seen that?"

"I've heard about it. But you're not straight."

"We were role-playing."

"You played straight?"

"I've taken acting classes. One thing led to another, and I end up with this." He pointed to his head. "It was supposed to be marmalade, but it looks like someone dipped my head in Jell-O.”

“Marmalade?”

“What about it?”

“Nothing. Your hair looks fine.”

Max smirked. “Don’t lie to me, Mister I-Hooked-Up-With-Erika.”

I glanced around the bar. His voice was way too loud.

He leaned in. “I saw you two talking. She’s got big eyes for you.” He lifted his chin at me. “Here she comes. Heed my words. The girl is swooning something fierce.”

A hand slid around my waist, and Max headed toward the other end of the bar.

I turned and faced Erika, whose smile held no secrets. “What are you doing here?”

“Checking in with Bosco.”

She jutted out her hip. “And I thought maybe you came to see me.”

“I wanted to give you some space.”

“When’s the last time you’ve courted a woman?”

“Erika!” Bosco called.

We both looked in his direction. He motioned toward the delivery driver. “Come. Help this man.”

She said, “Gotta go. Call me,” and hurried off.

Bosco pointed to an area away from the bar, Erika, and the delivery man. We both walked until we met in a quiet portion of the club. “You are bouncing tomorrow night.” It wasn’t a question.

“If I need to cancel, can you get someone to cover?”

He studied my head. “You’ve had two nights off. Are you still hurt?”

“I’m better.”

“Then why cancel? It is not like you to miss work.”

"Personal reasons. If I get it resolved today, I'll let you know."

Bosco put his hands on his hips. "Okay, but Friday and Saturday, you be here. No excuses. You are the only one who keeps the people in line."

I pointed at the stitches in my head. "I didn't do very good last time."

He smirked. "You are a good bouncer but terrible negotiator. You negotiate against yourself."

"Friday and Saturday," I said. "I'll be here."

Bosco clapped my shoulder. "You are good now. Enough being lazy. Bad for the soul."

***

Outside the Claremont Apartments, Detective Gary Ackerman stood near his dusty patrol car. His dark suit was in stark contrast to the surrounding neighborhood. He casually sipped from a white Starbucks cup.

His car sat underneath a NO PARKING—COMMERCIAL LOADING ZONE sign. For some reason, it bugged me.

"You might get a parking ticket," I said.

"I'm on official business."

"That's convenient. I'm sure the parking enforcement officers love when they see you guys in these zones."

He shrugged. "We can park wherever necessary."

"The concept of necessity gets stretched to the limits, though."

"Did I do something to piss you off?"

"What are you talking about?"

"Did you get this resentful after you left the department? Or were you a self-loathing officer?"

He was the second person today to accuse me of bad feelings toward the cops. What vibe was I giving off? I waved my hand dismissively.

"No, seriously," Ackerman said. "What's up with you?"

Since he wanted to know, I said, "I look at things through the eyes of a citizen now."

"No, you don't. You're sour. Citizens don't think the way you do."

"You're kidding. You and your five-hundred-dollar suit are going to tell those of us who live here," I thumbed toward the Claremont, "how we think about the police?"

"My suit is off the rack." Ackerman put his coffee on the top of the car. "And the majority appreciate law enforcement in all capacities. They appreciate the need for it even if they run afoul of it via parking or speeding ticket."

"Via? Who says that?"

His eyes hardened. "Adults understand that a society needs the police."

"You've lost touch, Detective. Most people dislike— No. That's too soft. They *fucking* hate law enforcement. The only interaction they ever have with the cops is when some eager traffic cop stops them on the way to work. The citizen gets a ticket, and the cop smiles like an asshole while doing it. The citizen goes home and bitches about it to their family. No good P.R. comes from that."

"Police work isn't public relations. It's about doing what's right."

"That's why people like firemen better. They help. Cops punish. Which do you think is better marketing?"

Ackerman exhaled heavily. "You have a special way of pissing people off."

"I've heard."

He grabbed his coffee, considered sipping, but didn't.

I glanced up and down the street then returned my attention to him. He seemed like a decent guy, and I thought he would do his best to try and find Peyton's killer. My anger toward law enforcement wasn't his fault. "Listen. I'm sorry. What you're doing is important. I get that."

Bitterly, he said, "Thank you."

"I mean it, I'm sorry. I don't know why I'm giving off those vibes."

"I do."

I raised an eyebrow.

"You got fired from Seattle PD. That's going to leave a mark. I got fired from McDonald's when I was a teenager. I haven't had a Big Mac since."

"That's probably taking it too far."

"Probably, but I understand why you'd hold a grudge. But I don't fault other people for working at McDonald's or enjoying the occasional Quarter Pounder. Even though I prefer a Whammy from Dick's."

Now, he was talking about burgers, trying to be my friend. "Why are you here, Detective?"

"I wanted to see how you were doing."

"You waited outside on the off chance that I might come by?"

"I already went up to your unit and knocked. When the dog barked and you didn't answer, I came back down. I'm on a coffee break." He lifted his cup. "I thought I could stand out here, drink my single tall and enjoy the afternoon shade until I finished. If you showed up, great. If not, well, I got some quiet time."

"And you don't want to talk about the case?"

He shook his head.

"Okay, I give. Why are you *really* here?"

"I told you—to see how you were doing. A former cop has lost his way. I thought he could use a friend."

I opened my mouth to say something snarky but closed it. He didn't deserve it. I'd already given him a ration of shit, and he remained professional. Worse, he stayed nice. I looked at my boots. They probably could use a shine. "I'm good."

"And the dog?"

"He's good, too."

"You've still got my card? In case you want to talk or anything."

I nodded.

"All right, then."

Ackerman stepped into the street to head to the driver's side of the car. He stopped and turned back. "Have you decided to stay out of my investigation?"

I remained silent.

The detective pointed at me with his cup. "Please, don't screw up anything we can't undo. I want to catch this guy."

"I want you to catch him, too."

He walked around his car and opened the driver's side door. "I'm not the enemy, John."

"I know."

Ackerman shot me a questioning glance before dropping into his car.

Chapter 19

I waited as patiently as I could inside my apartment. What needed to happen next couldn't occur until later in the evening. Corporal lay panting on the kitchen's vinyl floor. It was probably cooler. The fan was turned outward in the window and sucked the hot air from the room.

My eyes grew heavy, so I took a break from *The Big Sleep* to work on a crossword puzzle from the newspaper. I don't usually do them but taking a nap in this heat didn't sound appealing.

What is a five-letter word for a mournful sound? I wondered. Starts with K.

I struggled for the answer, but my thoughts kept sneaking back to Wayne Sadler. There wasn't anything further I could do about him right now. I had to wait. Imagining possible outcomes wasted creative energy and added worry.

I moved onto the next question. Lou Gehrig's disease, for short. Three letters. I knew that one.

Around six, there was a light tapping on the door. Corporal lifted his head.

"John?" More tapping. "Are you home?"

Tanya Robertson smiled when I opened the door. She wore a simple black dress that highlighted her deeply tanned skin. In her left hand was a small clutch. "How come you didn't answer your phone?"

I pulled it from my pocket. I'd missed three calls. All were from Tanya. "I put it on silent."

"Weird. Who does that?" She stepped inside and

pointed at the dog. "What is that?"

"A dog."

"I know it's a dog. Why do you have one?"

"Because a friend was murdered."

She turned back to the hallway and pointed at the police tape covering Peyton's door. "There?" It was the same reaction Erika had.

"No. Elsewhere." I shut the door. "The police did a search warrant on his apartment. They taped it off in case they wanted to come back again."

"Oh." Her face relaxed. "So, you took his dog?"

"For the time being."

"Does he bite?"

"No more than I do. Why are you dressed up?"

"I'm on my way to a fundraiser."

"Got a hot date?"

She smirked. "It's for one of the charities I'm on the board of."

"You look nice."

"This old thing?" She tossed her clutch on the coffee table then twirled for me. When she stopped spinning, she laughed. "It's hot in here. Is it hot in here?"

"It's warm."

She pulled at the shoulders of her dress, and it fell to the floor around her heels. "That's better."

"When does this thing start?"

"In an hour."

***

Ninety minutes later, Tanya stood in the bathroom and stared at herself in the mirror. "It's so hot in here," she groaned.

"It wasn't so bad before we started."

"Look at my hair." A sheen of sweat covered her body as she tried to tease her hair back into place. "What am I going to do?"

"Take a shower."

"And start over? Are you crazy? I'd never make the fundraiser."

"Then stay here."

She shot me a look that told me I was overstepping my place. I slipped into a pair of shorts and picked up the crossword puzzle from the other room. I returned to the bed and watched her work. She was wiping herself down with a washcloth.

"I'm going to smell like sex."

"I didn't force you."

Tanya leaned into the mirror. "What did you say?"

"What's a five-letter word for a mournful sound?"

"I don't know. Can't you see I'm busy?"

She dampened the washcloth again and went over herself once more. She returned to the bedroom stark naked and shiny as hell. With her hands on her hips, she asked, "What's it start with?"

"Usually with you being naked."

"Cute. No, your word. What's it start with?"

"K."

"Knell," she said and left the room.

Knell? I'd never heard of it. Stupid, but it fit. I followed her out. "How'd you know that?"

She was already in her dress and slipping her feet into the heels. "Haven't you heard of a death knell? That's a sound played at a funeral or something." She leaned into me. "I've got to go."

"I know."

She kissed me—just a peck on the cheek—nothing like our earlier passion. "I'll call you later. Keep your phone on this time."

"Why? Are you coming back?"

Tanya shrugged. "If there's time." The door clicked closed behind her.

Maybe I should have told her I had things to do. I checked my watch. There were still many hours to kill. I could either work on the crossword puzzle or go back to reading my book.

Knell, I thought and balled up the puzzle. I would have never gotten that word.

Chapter 20

The Playground's parking lot was empty except for a heavily dented '76 Chevy Luv. Its yellow skin was rusted, and the tailgate was a distant memory.

The bartender from the previous night walked out of the building with two bags of trash. Doing his best to keep the sacks from hitting the ground, he shuffled over to the dumpster. He set both bags down then flipped up the lid. It banged loudly. Then he grunted each time he swung one of the heavy loads into the garbage bin. He slammed the lid shut and jumped back with a "Hooyah!"

While he made all that unnecessary noise, I moved so near that I could touch him on the shoulder.

He dug a pack of cigarettes out from the pocket of his loose jeans. After one was lit, he leaned his head back and exhaled a plume of smoke into the night sky.

"Got an extra one?" I asked.

The bartender spun wildly to face me.

I punched him. Not hard and not in the face, but enough to get his attention. It was only a left jab to the chest and not much to brag about, but the guy fell as if I caught him on the chin with an uppercut.

The cigarette he had been smoking stuck to his lip and hung like a long, white cold sore. He blinked several times before speaking. "What'd you do that for?"

"For calling your goons on me last time."

"But you were asking about—" He caught himself before saying any more.

I grabbed his shoulder and pulled him to his feet. "Let's go inside."

"Why?"

"It's safer."

"For who?"

I shoved him, and he stuttered forward. When he got his balance, he ran toward the door. I expected him to do that and kept pace with him. The bartender yanked open the door and turned around. I'm sure he had the idea of stepping back and pulling the door with him, thereby locking me outside. But this time, I hit him—hard and in the face. The first punch to the chest should have been a warning.

He took several steps backward with his arms windmilling in reverse. He bumped into a high table, knocking it over. He then kicked out the legs of a stool and landed on it sideways.

I pulled the bar's door closed and locked it behind me.

"Nuh," he grunted and rolled over to his knees and the balls of his feet. Blood ran from his nose.

"Now that we've established the ground rules," I said, "let's move forward like gentlemen."

"The fuck! You hit me."

"I have some questions."

His fingers gently touched his face. "I think you broke my nose."

"No, I didn't. What's your name?"

"I'm not telling you anything."

"I can hit you again."

His eyes widened. "Cliff. Cliff Coffey."

He wasn't lying about the first name. One of the goons had called him Cliff.

"Next question. What's Mitch's last name?"

Coffey simply stared at me.

"Right," I said and hit him with a roundhouse heel palm. Not as hard as I could have because he was kneeling and defenseless, but I couldn't let the guy just play dumb. There were ground rules to abide.

The bartender went sprawling across the metal stool. He rolled off, covered his head with both arms, and stared up between the opening.

"Hitting you down there is going to be hard," I said, "so I'm going to kick you instead. Just so you know."

"Pierce," he said. "His last name is Pierce. Stop hitting me, will ya?"

"Is Mitch short for Mitchell?"

"How the hell should I know?"

I kicked him.

"Ow! Goddamn it, stop it."

"Where's he at?"

"I don't know—"

I pulled my foot back.

"But I know where he'll be! Stop hitting me!"

Cocking my head, I asked, "Where will he be?"

"Making a deal at three."

We couldn't have rhymed that on purpose and now wasn't the time for a witty comment. I'm not sure if he would have gotten it anyway. I glanced at my watch. Three was less than an hour away.

"Where is this happening?"

"Riverside and Magnolia. Behind the burnt-out warehouse."

"Who's he meeting with?"

"I dunno."

I kicked him.

"Nuh!" Still on his back, he scooted away and held his

hands up in front of himself. "Stop it! I dunno the guy's name. I swear!"

I kicked him a second time.

"I swear to God! I don't know."

He wouldn't risk another kick by lying again.

"How did you know about this deal?"

Coffey repositioned himself onto an elbow. "Enough with the kicking. All right?"

I repeated my question. "How did you know—"

"We're partners."

"In what?"

"Running bud." That puzzle piece clicked with what One Tooth told me. "We bring it out of Canada, parcel it up and sell it off."

"How long have you been doing that?"

"A couple years."

I glanced around the bar. "You're running B.C. bud, and you're still bartending?"

Coffey clicked his tongue and tapped his chest. He said defensively, "I own this place. It's mine."

"What's Mitch get out of this?"

"Nothing. It's mine." He seemed to have hurt feelings.

I took another look around. "Got a storage closet in this joint?"

He pointed toward the back of the bar.

"Get up."

Unsteadily, Coffey made it to his feet. He staggered like a drunk and had to use the wall to steady himself. He stopped in front of a door and pointed at it.

Inside was a mop and bucket along with the standard cleaning supplies. The room smelled like disinfectant and was the cleanest portion of the bar.

"Turn your pockets inside out."

The bartender did what he was told. A set of keys, a small wad of bills, and a cell phone all fell to the floor.

I motioned toward the closet. "Get in."

He flared his shoulders. "What if I don't—"

I punched him in the chest. "Nuh!" He collapsed onto the mop and bucket.

"If you manage to get out," I said, "what are you going to do?"

Coffey rubbed his jaw. "I'm not gonna do nothing."

"Because if you call Mitch and tell him I'm on the way—"

"He'll know I'm a rat."

"You could always tell him that I beat the truth out of you."

He rolled his eyes. "He won't ever trust me again."

"And if you call the cops—"

"Fuck the cops."

"Right answer."

After shutting the door, I pulled a chair over. With a shove, I wedged it under the doorknob. I'm not sure how long the thing would hold, but maybe it would slow him down, and maybe he would keep his word on not calling Sadler. I was betting on a couple of maybes.

I picked up Coffey's keys and threw them across the room. He'd at least have to search for them. The wad of bills remained where they were. I was many things, but a thief wasn't one of them. With the heel of my boot, I crushed the cell phone. There was still the landline behind the bar, and there might have been a phone elsewhere. I didn't have the time to search every place the man might be able to call from. Sooner or later, he'd be able to contact his partner. That was life. I just had to believe he would see the futility in doing so.

My truck was parked a couple of blocks away, and I sprinted the entire distance. There was less than forty minutes before Wayne Sadler's deal was set to go down. That was cutting it close, but I wasn't going to miss my chance to catch Peyton's killer.

Chapter 21

The meeting point at Riverside Avenue and Magnolia Street was in a dirt parking lot behind an abandoned warehouse. No lights illuminated the parking lot, but the partial moon provided enough to see everything.

Along the east side of the property, a row of overgrown shrubs ran the lot's length. I crouched near these bushes and waited.

I'd pulled a dark hooded sweatshirt from behind the seat of my truck and slipped it on. Even though it was warm, clandestine work required that I cover the pale skin of my arms.

Before leaving my vehicle, I flipped open my cell phone. I still had a few minutes left and about fifty percent power. I slipped it into the pocket of the hoodie.

My gun was tucked into the back of my jeans.

A newer white Ford Mustang sat backed up to the abandoned warehouse. Its lights were off, and its engine ran. There was no front license plate on the vehicle. Every few seconds, a cherry ember of a cigarette glowed brightly from the driver's seat. Even so, I couldn't make out the driver. Was it Wayne Sadler?

The cherry ember flared once more. I wanted a cigarette but knew better. I didn't want to give anyone the same advantage that the driver had given me.

A smell of fresh dog feces and rotting garbage drifted in from somewhere nearby. This area was a mixture of light industrial, small office buildings, and run-down residential homes. It didn't make for a flattering postcard.

Another car entered the neighborhood. Its engine was almost silent, and I failed to recognize it at first. When I did, it sounded as if it were coming up Magnolia behind me. I pushed into the bushes. The driver of the Mustang couldn't see me, but the driver of the unknown car might. I leaned deeper in and fell entirely off-balance. I grabbed onto the branches to stop from falling to the ground. The shrubs scratched my face and neck, but there was nothing else I could do. Pulling myself out of the shrubs now would alert the oncoming driver to my whereabouts.

I had put myself in a horrible position by assuming the next car would come in off Magnolia, an arterial.

Headlights swung from Pittsburg Street, lighting up the neighborhood, but they suddenly clicked off. A car drove slowly by. Looking over my shoulder, I could see a newer Mazda with door scoops and a tail fin. In the low light, the car appeared to be completely black, and the windshields were darkened. Once it passed by, I awkwardly climbed out of the bushes.

I moved forward a few feet and crouched behind a couple of smaller shrubs to get a better look.

The Mazda stopped next to the Mustang. Both the driver's and passenger's doors of the Mazda opened, and two men got out. The driver was a fat white guy who wore a Denver Nuggets jersey. The passenger was a Rastafarian with long dreadlocks and a club shirt.

The driver's door of the Ford opened. Even in the low light, I could tell it was Wayne Sadler. I'd stared at his picture enough recently to know. His hair was longish, and he wore a tank top and blue jeans.

It was time to call the cops. I reached for my phone. Gone.

I patted my pockets as Sadler stepped over to the other men.

My cell phone must have fallen into the shrubs. Turning around now and hunting for it in the dark wasn't an option. I screwed up. There was no other way to look at it. Had I put the phone in my front pocket instead of the hoodie, this wouldn't have happened. Instead, I crouched alone in the darkness, trying to determine how to apprehend Wayne Sadler.

Maybe I should let him drive away and just get the license plate number of his car. I could almost read the plate of the Mazda. I patted my pockets. I'd left my notebook and pen in the truck. This wasn't my finest moment.

The Rastafarian approached Sadler. "Mitch, brother."

"Badrick, my man."

Voices carry in the night, and I heard the two men from where I hid.

While Badrick and Sadler spoke, the fat man wandered to the edge of the parking lot. He never looked back to the others but instead scanned the surrounding area. His eyes studied the shrubs I was near.

My heart thumped wildly in my chest, and I crouched lower. Was the hoodie over my head enough to hide my face and make me look like a bush in the night?

The two men shook hands, but Badrick didn't release Sadler. Instead, he pulled him closer.

"Your face," Badrick said. "What happened?"

"Nothing."

The Rastafarian studied Sadler. "Looks like something."

"It wasn't about our business. Just some old trouble over a woman."

Badrick let go of Sadler's hand. "Women troubles led to business troubles."

A small chirp emanated, and Sadler pulled his cell phone from his jeans.

"What is this?" Badrick asked with suspicion clearly in his voice.

"It's my partner."

"We are in the middle of a deal."

Sadler lifted a finger to tell him to wait.

The fat man leaned slightly forward as he studied the bushes that I hid behind. It seemed he took a deep interest in where I was. I thought I was low enough and in a dark shadow. Perhaps, I'd thought wrong. The only way to get lower was to drop to my stomach but doing so would create motion—motion that would be seen.

"What?" Sadler said into the phone.

"We are in the middle of a deal," Badrick repeated, not happy at having to do so.

"When?" Sadler asked. His voice rose with concern.

"Now," Badrick said and pointed at the ground. "We are dealing now."

"Gimme a minute," Sadler snapped at the Rastafarian. "Goddamnit."

Offended, Badrick pulled back.

Sadler covered his open ear with his hand and turned away from the Rastafarian. "Say that again, Cliff."

Coffey *had* called Sadler.

The fat man pointed in my direction. "Yo."

Sadler slammed his phone shut, spun frantically, then backed toward his car.

"Where are you going?" the Badrick asked.

"Deal's off," Sadler said.

"The hell it is. You know how hard we have to work to get this stuff down here?"

The fat man lifted his jersey and pulled out a gun. He pointed it in my direction. "Yo, B."

"Is this about your woman problems?" Badrick asked.

Sadler frantically waved a hand. "You don't understand."

"I understand if you get in that car, we're gonna have a problem." Badrick lifted a gun at Sadler. "I want my money."

"Yo, B!" the fat man said.

"What?" Badrick barked.

"Ambush!" The fat man fired in my direction. I fell back, rolled along the sidewalk, and ran. Turning and getting into a gun battle with no cover and zero concealment was suicide.

Gunfire erupted as I sprinted away. Several rounds zipped by me, but I didn't bother to go for my truck. It was parked in the opposite direction. That would require a double back, and I wasn't willing to do that.

My priority was to find some concealment. Something that provided cover would be better. As I ran, I awkwardly tugged my gun from the back of my pants.

I found what I was looking for a block away—a slightly elevated porch attached to a rundown home. The deck was held in place with concrete pilings. I dove for the ground, low-crawled underneath, and hid. I didn't know what creepy crawly things might be under there, but they had to be better than men with guns. Snakes aren't prevalent in the city of Spokane, so I wasn't worried about getting bit by one of them.

I sucked for air and lay as quiet as possible.

In the middle of my second inhale, there was a single shot fired in the distance. I held my breath, and a second shot fired. I exhaled as slowly and quietly as possible. My lungs ached and sweat burned into my eyes.

Tires screeched before the sound of a racing engine faded into the night.

I waited to hear a second engine, but it never came. Perhaps the second driver had more sense than squealing out of the parking lot. But after all that gunfire, what would the extra noise matter?

An internal argument began of whether to return to the abandoned warehouse or let it be. What would I do if the cops showed up? I'd have to explain what I was doing out at three in the morning. There weren't many viable reasons for anyone to be wandering around at that time of night. And if I had to admit that I was in the middle of one of their investigations, then that might lead back to a bartender I assaulted. That action would be tough to defend.

After some time, I crawled out from underneath the porch. With incredible stiffness, I stood, shoved my gun into the back of my jeans, and dusted myself off.

A shotgun racked, and I froze.

"Just what the hell were you doing under my porch, boy?" The voice sounded older but strong enough to be trouble. "Turn around nice and slow. Don't try nothing foolish."

I raised my hands high in the air before turning around. An older man dressed only in white boxer shorts tucked a shotgun into his shoulder.

"It's not what you think," I said.

The man appeared to be in his seventies, and a paunch hung over his undershorts' waistband. "You better not be the sumbitch who broke into my truck."

"No, sir. That wasn't me."

The man traced the shotgun up and down my length. It was a frightening experience.

"You out doing pervert things then?"

"No, sir. I was hiding."

"From what?"

"Did you hear the gunshots?"

He aimed the shotgun at my face. "Was you part of them?"

Reflexively, I turned away. "No, sir! Please stop pointing that at me."

"What were you doing then?"

"Passing by."

"No man is passing by in this neighborhood. Try again."

"I'm looking for my daughter." It was a fast lie, but one I thought may carry some weight.

The shotgun lowered slightly. "Why didn't you say that in the first place?"

"Because I'm scared." There was no better time for the truth.

"Huh." He pointed the weapon to the side. Not much, but enough. "Any luck on her whereabouts?"

"No, sir."

"Good luck with that," he muttered and headed into his house. The door swung closed behind him.

I hurried to my truck. I considered taking the long way to avoid going by the abandoned warehouse, but there were no sirens yet. Maybe no one had bothered to call in the gunshots.

When I rounded the corner of Riverside and Magnolia, the Mazda remained in the parking lot. Near the driver's door, the Rastafarian lay face down. The fat man was in the middle of the street. I checked them both out and confirmed my suspicion on the last two shots. Each man had been wounded in the torso but had received a kill shot to the head. Sadler made sure they were dead and couldn't rat him out.

I sprinted back to my truck and fled the area.

Chapter 22

The next morning, I woke up with a splitting headache. I swung my legs off the side of the bed and sat upright with a groan. Corporal came over to see what my problem was. The way his tail wagged made it seem like he had no sympathy.

"Your breath stinks."

Unfazed by my critique, he continued to pant.

After swallowing a few aspirin, I took the dog for a walk. He relieved himself in a nearby parking lot. I didn't bring a poop bag again. Let the city sue me, I thought. It was a bad morning.

We returned to the apartment where I showered and shaved.

I hadn't called the police to report the previous night's shooting. Was it wrong not to? Yeah. Totally. There was no way to pretend it wasn't. But calling to say that I'd learned certain things would put me in the crosshairs of a certain detective. He might be a nice guy, but if he knew I was at the scene of a double murder and didn't report it—well, there was only so far that being nice would go.

Neither of the deceased were upstanding citizens. Of course, that was an assumption, and I was getting in trouble for making those lately. However, a couple of guys meeting with Wayne Sadler at three in the morning didn't scream Rotary Club. The local cops probably knew them. Or if they were Canadian, maybe they were known by the Mounties. If those guys had been citizens, I would have alerted the police.

Didn't they deserve the same protection as the rest of society?

Tell it to Peyton, I thought.

Tell it to his family.

Until then, I was going to keep what I saw to myself.

After a breakfast of cold cereal and a slightly mushy apple, I took the dog over to Riverfront Park. He'd already done his morning business, but this was to let him run and stretch his legs.

Corporal and I walked to our favorite spot. I unleashed him, and he did that same goofy run. Around in circles he went before trotting off into a cluster of trees.

I sat on the grassy hillside and stared at the backside of the Spokane Convention Center. The Spokane River ran between the building and the park.

At that moment, no one was in that area beyond us. That seemed normal since there were no rides or attractions where I sat. The park's central portion held the Looff Carrousel, the bike rentals, gondola ride, and snack stands. That was the area that everyone visited, and it already had a fair amount of people soaking up the midmorning sun.

Corporal loped toward me with his tongue hanging out and a bounce in his step. The dog stopped ten feet from me and went rigid. His lip curled, and he growled.

I glanced over my shoulder and saw a mountain of a man running in my direction. His face contorted in anger. It took a moment to comprehend the picture, but I rolled in the grass toward Corporal when I did.

The dog snapped and barked as I stood.

Houston, Rosa's boyfriend, stopped a few feet from us.

"Order arms," I said to the Shepherd. Corporal immediately stopped barking but kept his eyes trained on the big man. "What do you want?"

Houston sucked for air. He lifted weights, but the man struggled to breathe. For a moment, I thought about hitting him. But I'd been in enough fights to know that an out-of-breath Houston could still hurt me.

In between ragged breaths, he said, "Stay away… from her." He stepped forward and watched Corporal with evil eyes. "I ain't afraid of that dog."

"Go home, Houston."

His eyes snapped to me. "She told you my name?"

"Go home. You don't want this."

He clenched his fists. "Touch her, and you die."

I backed up, but the dog stayed put.

"I never touched her," I said.

His face reddened, and veins popped out on his forehead. "Stay away, or I'll make sure you do." Houston turned and walked away with occasional glances over his shoulder.

Chapter 23

"Is that dog under control?" Detective Ackerman stood in the hallway and watched the Shepherd lying in the middle of the apartment.

"He's fine. Come in."

When the detective stepped inside, Corporal got to his feet.

"What's he doing now?" Ackerman asked.

"I don't know," I said and closed the door.

The detective took a reflexive step back and bumped into the now-closed door. "Call him."

Corporal came forward, sniffed the detective's shoe, then his leg, before moving to his crotch.

"Don't move," I said. "Be very still."

Ackerman whispered from the side of his mouth, "Are you serious?"

"If you spook him, you might lose a testicle."

The detective held his hands out in the air. "Nice doggy. Good doggy." His voice was strained.

Corporal made a dismissive snort into Ackerman's groin, then moved to the center of the room where he flopped down.

"Does he greet all your guests that way?"

"Just you."

"That was uncomfortable."

"Then he's earning his keep."

Ackerman motioned toward the couch. "Mind if I sit?" He moved without waiting for my approval. "I get the feeling you're not being straight with me."

I crossed my arms and studied him. "How so?"

"It's a hunch. A cop's instinct. Is there anything you'd like to get off your chest?"

I slipped a cigarette from the Marlboro pack then leaned against the wall next to the window. The box fan whirred as it pulled the warm air from the apartment. "Is this on the record?"

"Of course, it's on the record. Everything about this is on the record."

I lit my cigarette and exhaled into the fan. It pulled the smoke outside. "Then I got nothing to say."

He snapped his fingers. "I knew it. You're messing around in my investigation."

"You already knew I was. I thought you gave me tacit permission."

He pointed at me and scowled. No more Mr. Nice Guy, I guess.

"Are we off the record?" I asked.

"No, damn it. We're still on the record. Tell me what you're doing."

"Why don't you start by sharing what you've got?"

His eyes narrowed. "I'm not sharing the status of my invest—"

"You think Peyton was killed randomly."

He shrugged.

"Serious?" I said. "How could you even think that?"

"I have to be open to it. In the same way, I must consider your lead on Wayne Sadler. Maybe someone else wanted your friend dead. Have you thought of that? We have to look at more possibilities than—"

"It was Sadler," I said.

"I don't have the luxury to be myopic."

"Myopic."

"It means—"

"I know what it means." I inhaled deeply on my cigarette.

The detective was pissing me off. He should have spent his time and energy getting after Wayne Sadler, but instead, he was chasing ghosts. There was no way that Peyton was the victim of a random killing. Someone had beat the man to death in broad daylight. If it happened at night in a dark corner, I could have believed it random but not in the circumstances it played out.

No, there was one guy Peyton crossed, and that guy was Wayne Sadler. And the detective was wasting his resources.

"It was Wayne Sadler," I said sternly. "Trust me."

"And now you're going to tell me you've had some luck finding this guy? Is he hanging out somewhere with D.B. Cooper?"

I rolled the cigarette between my thumb and forefinger. "Off the record?"

Ackerman moved his head around his shoulders. "Fine. Whatever. It's off the record."

"Then I found him."

"*Bullshit!*"

Startled, Corporal jumped to his feet and growled.

"At ease," I said. The dog sat but continued observing the detective.

Ackerman spoke, but his eyes remained on Corporal. "So, where is the elusive Mr. Sadler?"

I crushed out my cigarette. "I don't know."

The detective rubbed his face. Next, he ran his fingers through his hair, mussing it slightly. "You found him, but you don't know where he is?"

"That's right."

"That doesn't make sense. Start at the beginning."

"He's connected to the Playground."

"The bar up in Dog Town?" Ackerman frowned. "How did you find this out?"

"Talking with people."

"And they willingly offered up this information?"

"Some might have taken some encouragement."

"This encouragement wouldn't include threats of violence, would it?"

I turned my palms up in a what-can-I-say gesture.

"It better not have included actual violence. Because actual or implied makes their information coerced and inadmissible."

"I'm not a cop."

"I know, but if it ever goes to court—"

"That's why this is off the record."

Ackerman looked down and puffed his cheeks as he expelled a long breath of air. When his gaze returned to me, he asked, "Who were these people?"

If I told him names, he'd interview them. He seemed like a sharp detective, and that's what those types do—they follow up on things. If Cliff Coffey wanted to press charges, I was looking at a felony. I'd assaulted him inside his establishment. "I can't say."

"We're off the record," he reminded me.

"But if I give you a name, you'll interview them—on the record. Then those threats of violence…" I let the rest of it hang in the air.

"Or acts of violence." He didn't let it hang.

"If there was such a thing."

"That comes back to haunt you."

"Right now, nobody seems too worried about reporting any threats or acts."

"If such a thing were to have occurred," he said. He interlaced his fingers and tapped his thumbs together. "So, all I get is some nebulous bullshit that Wayne Sadler exists."

"I got a name."

"You just said—"

"Sadler's assumed name—the one he's been living under."

Ackerman's face flattened.

"Mitch Pierce, probably short for Mitchell, but I couldn't get that confirmed."

"This is back on the record." He pulled a pen and notebook from his suit coat. When he finished making the entry, he said, "Anything else?"

"Sadler's running marijuana out of Canada."

The detective glibly waved his hand. "Bullshit. The guy is wanted for vehicular homicide and fleeing. He's not going to risk getting caught dealing dope. What about his parents? They bonded him out years ago. They could be funding his life in exile."

"And maybe they're not. Maybe they thought they were doing the right thing by bonding out their baby boy. Maybe they didn't expect him to run, so they cut him off from the family fortune."

"That's a lot of maybes."

He had a point. I was doing that a lot lately.

"Can you track them down?" I asked. "Unless you want me to run over to Montana. They might have moved since then."

Ackerman seemed to think about that. "Yeah." He tapped his notepad. "I can do that."

"In light of all those maybes, is running dope so farfetched? It's not like he can get a real job. And his brain works differently than yours or mine. He's got to think that he's smarter than the law since he hasn't been caught yet. Whatever he has been thinking, he's scared now."

"Why do you say that?"

I crossed my arms and stared at him.

Ackerman considered his notepad. He closed it and tucked it back into his coat pocket. "Off the record."

"Remember that."

"How am I going to forget? I just said it."

"Two people were murdered last night. Wayne Sadler was there."

Ackerman leaned forward. "There are—" His fists balled, and his face reddened. "There are two detectives and a forensic unit out *right now* with a double homicide. Riverside and Magnolia. An abandoned warehouse."

"They're drug dealers."

"How could you possibly know that?"

As I replayed the scene from the night before, Ackerman's fists opened and closed. I avoided telling him about the older man who held the shotgun on me. Doing so would have given him a way to verify that I was out there. I didn't expect Ackerman to double-cross me, but I shouldn't hand him a witness to my actions either. When I finished my story, the detective looked away and clenched his fists a final time.

"You should have called nine-one-one." His voice was low, but anger bubbled under the surface.

"I couldn't do that."

"You witnessed a *homicide*," he snapped.

Corporal raised his head from the floor and watched the detective.

"I didn't witness anything."

"Yes, you did."

"No, I witnessed two cars pull into the parking lot of an abandoned warehouse. I suspected it to be a drug deal. I didn't see money or product change hands. Then a man I suspected to be a bodyguard shot at me. I fled the area. I heard shots. I didn't see anything. When I returned, two men were dead."

"You put two and two together. Sadler killed them."

"He did? Maybe he had back-up in his car. Maybe he had help around the corner. Maybe they were ambushed by rival dealers."

"You and your maybes," the detective said humorously.

"You're the one who said I should be open to more than one possibility."

"You still should have called the cops."

"I lost my phone." I wasn't worried about the forensic unit finding it at the crime scene. It was a burner, and nothing was registered to my name. For once, being poor was going to pay off dividends. Unless they printed it, I thought. But my fingerprints wouldn't prove I killed anyone—only that I had been in the vicinity at some time.

"You could have called from a payphone."

I crossed my arms. "What would that have done?"

"Are you kidding? It would have gotten us out there sooner. Our department wasted valuable time with no suspects when they could have been chasing Sadler."

"What is the first question they would ask me?"

Ackerman's eyes flicked away. "They'd ask what you were doing out at that hour."

"That's the easy question. What's the hard one?"

His gaze returned to me. It took him a moment to land on it. When he did, he said, "They'd want to know how you found the drug deal."

"And I'd have to lie, or I'd have to tell them about the

guy who gave me the coerced information."

"Threats of violence?"

"I probably would have called if all I did was threaten him."

Ackerman's hand dropped to his knees. "This is a mess." He stood and smoothed out his slacks. Corporal hopped up into an alert position. "That dog gives me the creeps."

"Think what you're giving him."

"Stay away from the investigation."

"Are you working Peyton's case full time?"

"I'm doing the best I can."

"How many other open cases do you have?"

"That's irrelevant," Ackerman said.

"It's not irrelevant. I can imagine the caseload you have. I know how things work."

"I'll put some patrol guys on it. Maybe even grab a couple guys from the general dicks pool."

"You think those guys will give a damn about Peyton?"

"They'll do their job," Ackerman said, his voice challenging.

"Not like I will. I want to find Sadler because he killed my friend."

Ackerman stared at me. We fell silent as we watched each other. The only sounds were the laboring of the overworked fan and Corporal's panting.

Finally, the detective said, "You're giving me heartburn."

He closed the door behind him.

Chapter 24

"Where were you last night?" Erika asked. She stood near my booth at the Satellite Diner. She wore a tight white t-shirt, black shorts, and white sandals. "I stopped by your apartment, but you weren't there."

"How'd you know I was here?"

"You talk about this place." The way she said it had an air of finality to it. She slid into the booth. "Now, answer my question."

I set down my sandwich and wiped my hands with a napkin. "I'm not sure why I need to do that."

Her mouth hung open for a moment before she said, "You're kidding, right?"

"No."

"You and me. We—"

"We what?"

Embarrassed, she looked around. She whispered, "I thought it meant something."

"It did."

"I don't do that with just anybody. Do you?"

I wiped my hands some more because I didn't know what else to do. There was no way I was telling her about Tanya.

"I'm not a whore," she said.

"I didn't say you were."

She'd already told me that the first night, which meant she must be worried about being seen that way.

"You might not be saying it," she said, "but you're treating me like one."

"I didn't mean to."

Her tongue peeked out between her lips, and she bit it.

"Can we start again?" I asked. I motioned toward her. "Please sit down."

"I'm already sitting."

"I know." I smiled. "I'm trying to start over."

She shook her head. "I don't want to play games. Where were you last night?"

"I was working."

"No, you weren't. I *was* working." Her look was intense. "Why won't you tell me where you were?"

"Erika, I do other things beyond bouncing at the club."

"I know you do, but at two-thirty in the morning?"

Would it hurt to tell her? If she knew I was hunting for a fugitive, could anything blow back on her? The way she watched me showed that I'd have to be careful with her no matter what I said. She had feelings way too fast.

"I was trying to find a guy."

She rested her arms on the table. "That doesn't tell me anything."

I leaned in and lowered my voice. "This guy might have something to do with my friend's murder."

Her eyes widened. "Why are—" Her brow furrowed, and she nervously licked her upper lip. "Is this something you can get hurt doing?"

"Not if I'm careful."

"Why are you doing that?"

I took a bite of my grilled ham and cheese.

"I want to know. I'll wait until you finish chewing."

When I swallowed, I said, "He was my friend. I don't need any reason beyond that."

She watched me eat another bite. She started to slide out of the booth but stopped. She moved back to where she was before. "I don't get you."

"What's to get?"

"I thought you liked me."

"I do."

"I mean, really liked me. I thought that's why we did what we did."

I tossed the remaining bit of sandwich onto my plate. "I like you."

"But?"

"You can do better than me."

She rolled her eyes. "Please, don't. If you don't want to see me, just say it."

"I'm not an idiot. With you, I've outkicked my coverage."

"I don't know what that means."

"It means you're out of my league. You can get a more handsome guy, a guy with some money."

"But I like you."

I sighed. "Maybe I'm not good enough for you."

"My father says when a man tells you he's not good enough, I should believe him."

"He sounds wise."

"Not always. Listen, I gotta go." She was halfway out of the booth but stopped again. "Bosco scratched you from the schedule tonight."

"Yeah, I called him."

"Why? Are you going after that guy again?"

I nodded.

"I'll come by when I get off."

"What if I'm not there?"

"Then call me and tell me where you are."

"I lost my phone."

"That better not be an excuse."

I lifted my hand. "Scout's honor."

"That's not how you do it." Her eyes narrowed. "You do realize I'm throwing myself at you, don't you?"

I nodded.

"So long as you realize it."

She left the diner then.

How stupid was I? I should do anything to be with her, but I knew where it would go if I gave in. I'd fall for her, and sooner or later, she would tire of me. Then I would be the one pining away.

It was bad enough with Tanya, and I knew damn well there was no future in that. Erika held the allure of possibilities.

But she was a mirage. They all were.

Chapter 25

The Playground had closed twenty minutes prior, and all the cars in the parking lot were now gone except a brown Volvo. The yellow Chevy Luv that I figured belonged to Cliff Coffey wasn't in the parking lot. Could he also own a Volvo? I didn't imagine Coffey driving a boxy European car.

I could have turned around and headed home, but I'd already wasted a day expecting to confront the man again. That was a mistake. Now, I needed to track him down away from the bar. Hopefully, whoever was working would be able to help me with that task.

My truck was again parked a couple of blocks away on a side street. It would have been too obvious for it to be in the lot with the Volvo. There was no convenient place to wait for the bartender to exit without being immediately seen. If the closing process were the same as the previous night, the bartender would soon bring out the trash.

I headed over and waited behind the dumpster. The smell of rotting food and sour beer was overpowering.

When the backdoor opened, a woman exited. She was a thin woman with short blonde hair. She wore a black t-shirt, faded blue jeans, and dirty red Converse tennis shoes. She pushed a concrete block in front of the door to hold it open. She returned inside the building.

I thought about going then, but the movement of shadows and light inside the bar gave me pause. She headed out again. The woman carried two bags of trash. As she waddled from the weight of the garbage, she gasped with every couple of steps. However, she was picking up steam. The heft of the trash propelled her forward.

Force equals mass plus acceleration, I thought. Or was that mass times acceleration? I didn't have time to pretend to ponder the problem any further because the woman stopped at the dumpster and dropped the bags.

"Ugh," she groaned.

She righted herself, then stretched her back. From where I hid, I could see the Playground's logo on her t-shirt. She wheezed as she reached for the container's lid.

I stepped from behind the dumpster. "Need some help?"

"Christ!" she screamed and lifted her arms to protect herself. "Take what you want."

"Relax."

She peered at me through the arms covering her head. One leg was lifted and twisted around the other.

"I'm not going to hurt you," I said.

"What do you want?" Her voice was raspy.

"Where's Cliff?"

Her leg lowered, but she kept her arms up around her head. "He called in sick."

"An owner calling in sick. That's convenient."

She dropped her arms. Now, I could see her face. She was in her mid-fifties and had the sallow skin of a long-time graveyard worker. "He told you he was the owner?"

"Yeah."

She kicked a hole in one of the trash bags. "Goddamn him. Stupid, lying bastard." The woman put her hands on her hips, pursed her lips, and glared at me.

"I take it you're the owner."

"What gave you that idea?"

I pointed at her scowl.

"Son of a bitch!" That seemed to snap her out of it, and

she waved an apologetic hand. "Son of a bitch," she repeated softly.

"He's claimed to be the owner before?"

"Usually, it's with some bimbo he's trying to shag, but yeah." She eyed me. "He wasn't trying to shag you, was he?"

"No."

"I'm not judging."

"No," I repeated and lifted the lid of the dumpster.

She stepped back and asked suspiciously, "What are you doing?"

"Throwing your trash away."

"*Why?*"

"I was being nice, but if you want—"

She motioned toward the bags. "By all means."

Carefully, I lifted the torn bag into the container. The second bag followed. After closing the lid, I wiped my hands against each other.

"What do you want with Cliff?" she asked.

"To talk."

"About?"

"The men he's gotten himself mixed up with."

She frowned. "This wouldn't have anything to do with the police presence we had tonight?"

"It might. What kind of attention were you getting?"

"Patrol walk-throughs. We hardly ever get those. Usually on New Year's Eve or St. Patrick's Day, but that thing is only for show, so the boys in blue can justify their overtime pay. Got to say, at first, the customers were concerned, but after the third visit, folks were getting into it. Betting on which regular the cops were after. Guessing what crime might bring that much attention. That sort of thing."

"The uniforms never said who they were looking for?"

"You know how cops are—all secretive and arrogant. They came in and gave us the growly face. They ID'd some of my customers. Just to be dicks, I think, then they left."

"You said three visit—"

"At least."

"In all that time, the cops never said who they were looking for?"

"No." Something in the way her eyes flared gave it away.

"But you know."

"I know."

"How?"

"A detective came in—all smooth and under the radar. No one even realized he was there. The guy looked like he'd just gotten off some shift at the factory."

Was she describing Ackerman? I couldn't imagine the detective out of suit looking the way she said. Maybe he had help.

She continued. "We chatted for a bit about nothing in particular, and then he showed me a picture. Palmed it so no one could see." She mimed the action.

"He give you a name?"

"Wayne. I'd seen him around a time or two, but I don't think that's his name."

"Did you give the detective any more info than that?"

She eyed me.

"I'm not with Wayne."

Her eyes narrowed further.

"And I'm not going to hurt you."

"I wouldn't think so. A man doesn't throw a woman's trash away then hurt her. Unless, of course, he's some sort of sicko, but I don't think that's you." Her head cocked. "Where'd you get those stitches?"

"Beer bottle."

"The man everyone is looking for—this Wayne—did he hit you with that bottle? The detective wouldn't tell me what he did. He just said he was wanted."

"Wayne murdered my friend."

She swallowed. "Was Cliff involved?"

"I don't think so."

"He couldn't." She lowered her head. "He wouldn't."

"I only want to talk to Cliff so he can tell me how to find Wayne."

"And you're sure he knows him?"

"I am."

Disappointment entered her eyes. "One hundred percent?"

"Cliff already told me how to find him, but Wayne gave me the slip."

She sighed then stared off into the night sky. It seemed as if she was battling with a decision. When her gaze fell from the heavens, she said, "Wait here."

"Where are you going?"

"To get his address."

"I'll go with—"

"No." Her voice was stern. "You wait out here."

I wanted to follow her inside and go wherever she went, but I asked her to trust me. I needed to have trust in her.

She walked over to the door, pushed the concrete block away, and went inside. The door swung shut.

The night was quiet. An occasional car raced northbound on nearby Market Street. Somewhere a dog barked.

I wondered how long I should wait. A couple of

minutes. Three at the most. If she called the cops, what was the worst that would happen? They would come and ask me some questions. I hadn't assaulted her. Instead, I had helped her with her trash. What kind of trouble could I get for that?

If she called Coffey, he might tell her that I beat the hell out of him. In that case, maybe his three goons would be on the way back. How long would it take them to arrive? Unless they were in the neighborhood, it would take longer than two minutes.

Three at the most, I reminded myself.

Wayne Sadler wouldn't risk showing up. How did I know that? I couldn't make that assumption. He'd killed two men the previous night. He'd killed Peyton. He'd been on the run from justice for fifteen years. Who knew what he was willing to risk now?

The door swung open, and she stepped out. She absently waved a little white card as she approached. "Not that I should care but promise you won't hurt him."

"I want to find the man who killed my friend."

She either didn't care that I avoided a promise, or she made peace with my answer. She handed me the card. "Here's his address."

It was Clifford Coffey's alcohol server's permit issued by the Washington State Liquor Control Board. His address was on it and showed he lived in north Spokane County.

Unfortunately, I hadn't brought a notepad or had anything to write with. I studied the card. The woman watched as I mumbled the address. Repeating it, I tried to make it into a chant. I was about to repeat it a third time when she interrupted.

"What are you doing?"

"Trying to commit the address to memory."

"Take the card."

My brow furrowed.

"Like I need this trouble." She waved her hand. "Strange men are hiding in my parking lot. Cops are rolling through my bar looking for a murderer. As far as I'm concerned, Cliff is through working at my bar."

She spun on her heel and headed back toward the Playground.

"Thank you," I called.

"Whatever." She yanked open the door and went inside.

Chapter 26

Cliff Coffey lived on Dunlop Road in Deer Park, a town in northern Spokane County. Before leaving the city, I stopped for gas at a locally owned convenience store. While the pump ran, I went inside to buy a map. I had never been to Deer Park, so I would need some help to avoid driving aimlessly around.

I took Highway 395 north before dropping off on Staley Road. After only a moment on the backroad, the darkness of a country night soured my disposition. I flicked on my brights. I'm not a country boy. I like cities with streetlights at every corner. If that wasn't manly, I didn't care. There were certain conveniences I could do without—living at the Claremont proved that. However, light seemed to be one of the few amenities I didn't feel comfortable parting with.

Finding Dunlop Road proved tricky in the early morning darkness. There wasn't a road sign, and pine trees shrouded its entrance. When I passed it the first time, I grunted but didn't slam my brakes. If anyone was awake at that hour, there was no reason to alert them to my presence. I lowered my headlights and continued down the road for a bit. Eventually, I slowed and conducted a clumsy U-turn.

When I returned to Dunlop Road, I killed my lights entirely and drove slowly. The houses along this stretch seemed several acres apart. There was no easy way to determine house numbers except by using the mailboxes along the roadside. Due to the lack of light, though, I could barely read most of them. Reluctantly, I flicked the headlights back on.

Soon, I found a mailbox with spray-painted numbers that matched those listed on Coffey's liquor server's permit. Once more, I turned off the lights. I gently pulled to the side of the road when I found a stretch of trees that might provide concealment from occupants of the house.

Before leaving the truck, I removed my gun from the glovebox. This wasn't a time to rely solely on my communication skills.

The ranch-style home sat almost a hundred yards back from the road. I stayed away from the gravel driveway and crept along in overgrown grass and weeds. Near the house, a beat-up Chevy Luv was parked under a corrugated metal awning. Miscellaneous junk was scattered around the lean-to and the perimeter of the house.

Now that I was here, I faced a dilemma. Do I knock on the door and wake a sleeping Coffey? What if he wasn't snoozing and saw my approach? He could be armed and waiting for me. Perhaps he could have called the cops. Stranger things have happened, even if it seemed unlikely.

If I could find an unsecured opening, should I enter the house? That would be another felony. I'd already committed one when I broke into Peyton's apartment. I'd committed yet another when I assaulted Coffey at the Playground. What was the problem in adding a third?

The difference, I realized, was the gun cupped in my hands.

I stood hunkered at the edge of the house and tried to come to a decision.

This wasn't smart. I should have called Ackerman and let him deal with it. I should have kept my nose out of the investigation. None of this was my responsibility. What the hell was I doing here?

An image of Peyton lying on the gurney flashed through my consciousness.

Right, I thought. This was my business. Peyton was my friend. I was doing this because I could. Because I would devote more energy to it than anyone else.

I crept around the back and stopped when I heard an unmistakable sound—one I knew very well. Somewhere a box fan ran at full strength.

How could I hear it so clearly now? Another step forward revealed why. The backdoor was open, but an aluminum door with its screen missing remained in place. A box fan sat on a chair in the doorway and sucked the cool night air into the house.

I knocked on the aluminum doorframe. Its clatter was loud in the quiet of the night. I pulled back and raised my gun at the opening.

For a moment, no one answered.

When my courage returned, I knocked again and created more clatter. I yelled, "Yo, Cliff. It's me."

I raised my gun and waited. Several excruciating minutes passed. A bead of sweat rolled down my temple.

Gently, I pulled open the aluminum door. It rewarded my carefulness with a metallic squeal. I almost let go of the door as if it burned me, but I froze instead. In the other hand, the gun remained steady.

If no one had come yet after knocking, yelling, and that damn squeal, no one was going to. I had to repeat that to myself a couple of times to believe it. Either Cliff Coffey was the hardest sleeping man in the world, or he wasn't home. I put one foot across the threshold.

Or Coffey was dead, I thought. That stopped me cold.

Now, my nerve was almost gone. Part of me screamed

to turn around, to run back to my truck, and go home. I hadn't gone entirely into the house—only a step. A half-step since a portion of my body was still outside the house.

If Cliff Coffey was dead, I could claim some sort of ignorance if I turned around now. Thinking that bothered me. Someone killed my friend, and here I was ruminating about levels of knowledge so I could avoid facing my fears.

I set my jaw, lifted my gun, and stepped into the house. Adrenaline coursed through my veins. My breathing shallowed, and droplets of sweat cascaded down my back.

The inside of Coffey's house was worse than the outside. Garbage and debris were strewn about. A disassembled dirt bike sat in the middle of the living room. Newspapers were placed underneath several components, and a pile of tools rested nearby.

In the hallway, a clear plastic bag sat on a small dark wood table. I lifted the bag to the ambient light and saw a green leafy substance. I smiled humorously. When I was a cop, that's the way we identified marijuana in arrest reports so it would play well in court. I tossed the baggie onto the table and continued down the hall. No pictures adorned the walls.

At the first doorway, I peeked in and found a clean room with several Seattle Mariners posters on the walls. Toys were on the dresser, and a stuffed bear took up the middle of a neatly made bed.

The second door was for the bathroom. In the final room was a queen-sized bed with clothing scattered about. The funk of man hung heavy in the room.

Clifford Coffey wasn't home, and he wasn't dead.

I returned to the living room, sat on the couch, and let a series of thoughts run through my brain.

What kind of person leaves his house open with a fan running? Maybe they do that out in the country.

Where the hell was Coffey at three in the morning?

Wasn't that the same question that Erika had asked me earlier in the day? Or would that be yesterday now?

I chuckled at the thought then straightened. What the hell was I doing? I was in the middle of burglary, sitting in a stranger's home, thinking about Erika busting my chops. I needed my head examined.

This wasn't the time to sit and ponder. I was there for a mission—find info on Wayne Sadler. I stood with renewed purpose. I'd wasted enough time already and needed to double-time it now.

After finding a switch, I clicked on the living room's light. It looked worse illuminated, but I searched every piece of paper I could find. When I finished, I turned off the light and ran down the hallway to what I assumed was Coffey's bedroom. The only things I found there were beat-up *Hustler* magazines and an old copy of *Northwest Sportsman*.

Even though it was a long shot, I checked the kid's room. Its cleanliness stood in stark contrast to the rest of the house. Even the clothes were folded neatly in the drawers. A sketch pad sat on a chair in the corner. Written on the cover, in a child's scrawl, was the name Patrick Donnelly.

I was about to leave the house when I realized I hadn't searched the kitchen. Dirty dishes were piled high in both sinks. On the counter was a loose photograph of Coffey, Wayne Sadler, and a boy probably ten years old. They were outside the Spokane Indians ballpark. I slipped the picture into my pocket and continued my search.

It felt like I was missing something. I scanned the

kitchen once more. As an afterthought, I swung open the cabinet doors underneath the sink. There was a small blue trash can.

It took only a minute of digging to find something. Among statements for Coffey's cell phone, electricity, and house payments was an envelope addressed to Joseph Benzo. Inside was an invitation to attend the father and son doughnut breakfast at Kennedy Elementary. The breakfast was last week. I pulled out the photograph in my pocket and calculated the odds that the boy in the photo was Patrick Donnelly and Joseph Benzo was another alias for Wayne Sadler. The address on the envelope was in Spokane Valley.

I tucked the invitation and photograph into the envelope and stuck them into my back pocket. Then I put the garbage can back where it belonged, turned off the kitchen light, and hurried out of the house. As I trotted back to my truck, I stepped into a hole and fell into the weeds and overgrown grass. I didn't drop my gun, though.

In the cool of the dark morning sky, I lay there, happy to be out of Cliff Coffey's house. Nearby on Dunlop Road, an engine revved. Probably some country jackass with a souped-up truck. I figured I would stay where I was until the vehicle went by. Then I would get up and—

The noisy truck turned into Coffey's driveway and sped up to the house. It didn't slow as it raced by me. I rolled over in time to see a Ford Bronco slam its brakes right before the lean-to.

Fear lanced through me. Had they somehow known I was inside the house? Were there sensors somewhere I didn't see? Video cameras? I prepared to run.

When the engine quieted, four men climbed lazily from the rig. Even in the dim moonlight, I knew all of them—

Cliff Coffey, One Tooth, Twitchy, and Scarface.

"Son of a bitch, Tommy," Coffey yelled, "Who taught you to drive?"

"Your mom," someone quipped.

The group guffawed, and Coffey swore loudly. Then the four of them meandered toward the house. I low crawled until I heard the screech of the screen door. Then I stood and ran.

Chapter 27

After a few hours of sleep, I woke to hot, stinky breath in my face.

"Ugh," I muttered.

The dog jumped at my awakening and ran from the room. I closed my eyes and tried to go back to sleep. In a moment, the warm, smelly breath returned.

"The hell?" I groaned and opened a single eye.

Corporal paced back and forth then. From the end of the bed to my head, he went. His tail wasn't wagging.

"Do you want to go outside?" I asked.

Again, the dog ran from the room.

***

We barely made it to the nearby parking lot before the dog scrunched his body.

I looked away to give him privacy and made eye contact with a well-dressed woman passing by. She looked scornfully at the dog then went on her way.

When he finished, Corporal stepped forward and scratched the asphalt with his hind legs. I hadn't seen him do that before. "What's that for?"

The dog ignored my question and walked to the end of his leash. He left his mess behind for me to clean up. The two of us were in such a hurry to get out the door that I hadn't considered bringing a bag. I glanced around to make sure no one had watched the dog do his business.

Then we walked casually back inside the Claremont.

***

Back on the sixth floor, Peyton's apartment was open, and Corporal headed immediately for it. I reeled in his leash, and we both peered into the apartment.

An older woman in blue slacks and a shiny red blouse stood up from a box she was bent over. Helen Rudd was the manager for the Claremont Apartment.

With the weight of only a few hours of sleep, I asked, "What are you doing?"

"Packing Peyton's stuff. The coroner's office called and released the apartment. Since Peyton didn't list an emergency contact on his application, there's no one to get this stuff. We need to pack it and put it into storage. State requirements and such." Her gaze dropped to Corporal. "Are you keeping his dog?"

"I guess so."

"I'll note it in the file." Her smile seemed slightly uncomfortable.

"What's wrong?"

"We're supposed to get a pet deposit."

"Oh."

"Legally, we can't transfer Peyton's over to you. Auditors and accountants and such."

"Right."

"I'll just make a note in your file that you took his dog and see if no one at corporate notices."

"I'd appreciate that." I motioned toward the boxes. "Need some help?"

Helen smiled. "That would be nice."

"Let me put the dog away."

I led Corporal over to my unit. My eyes burned from a

lack of sleep, and my body felt heavy. Part of me wished I had kept my mouth closed and not volunteered. The other part didn't want the remnants of my friend's life to be unceremoniously stuffed into cardboard boxes.

Back in Peyton's apartment, Helen directed me to start in the kitchen. We chatted as we worked. Helen was in her early sixties and acted as sort of a den mother to the residents. Most of us appreciated what she did and were protective of her.

"Did you know Peyton long?" she asked.

"We met after I moved in. Took some time to warm up to each other."

"Residents come and go. He was a nice fella, though. Always respectful."

"Do you have to do this often? Clean an apartment after someone dies?"

She held a hardback book on Viet Nam, and her face tightened. "I've been here a lot of years. I've done it more than I care to remember. Sometimes, the person who is gone was not so nice—packing up after them is no harder than cleaning an apartment after someone moves out. Just get in, box everything up, and get out. Lickety-split."

Helen set the book into the box and picked up another book. It appeared to be another about war—there was a tank on the cover—but I couldn't make out its title. "Then there are people like Peyton. He was always kind. Helpful, too. Sometimes, he'd stop in at the end of the day, and we'd talk for an hour after I got off. He wasn't trying to get anything from me. Some of the men here think if they flirt a little— Well, you get what they're after."

I nodded.

"But not Peyton. He wasn't that type of man. He missed his family was all." We made eye contact. "Did he tell you what happened to his wife and daughter? It was a horrible thing—a tragedy. Something like that leaves scars that can't be seen, but they'll never be forgotten either."

I thought about a woman I once loved, but she never loved me back. It was a tumultuous relationship that ended with me hating her. Her murder washed the anger from my memory. All that was left was a feeling of forever loss. It was stupid to carry that kind of melancholy, but I couldn't seem to shake it.

Helen put the other book into the box. "It's kind of cathartic. Cleaning after they're gone." She found a framed picture of Peyton in his uniform and studied it. "It lets me remember the good stuff."

"I'm sure he would have wanted you to have it."

She frowned. "I can't. It's not right." She put the frame into a box. "There are rules. If you start breaking one, you end up breaking two. Then where does it stop? Besides, if I kept something from everyone who has ever died, my life would be filled with only reminders of loss."

Our conversation meandered after that, and we finished in about an hour. We carried the boxes into the hallway for the maintenance man to pick up with a handcart.

Helen touched my upper arm. "Thank you for helping, John."

I nodded and returned to my apartment. Once inside, I sat on the couch. The dog came over and put his head on my lap. He stared up at me while I stroked his fur.

We sat like that for several minutes until I fell asleep.

***

Shortly after noon, I awoke to a hammering on my door. I flopped off the couch and landed on all fours. Then I moved to the door where Corporal stood alert and ready.

When the door opened, Rosa jumped into my apartment and slammed the door shut behind her. "He's after me," she said breathlessly. "I couldn't go home." She spun around, locked the door, and slid the brass chain into place. She turned back to me and flopped against the door. A large red welt was on her cheek. Horizontal, purple streaks were on both sides of her neck.

Corporal sniffed her as she sucked for air. I pushed the dog away and pulled Rosa deeper into the apartment.

"Are you all right?" I asked.

She shook her head then bent at the waist. As she sucked for air, she sounded as if she were about to hyperventilate. I grabbed her hand and led her to the couch.

"Sit," I said, "and put your head between your legs."

Rosa's hands clasped her knees, and she anxiously rocked back and forth. When her breathing finally took on a familiar rhythm, she straightened.

"You're all right," I said, my voice encouraging.

Her eyes widened as she wrapped her arms around herself and tucked her legs underneath.

I softened my voice. "Tell me what happened."

"He caught me walking out of PM Jacoy's. I had two bags of groceries in my arms." She looked toward the ceiling and fought back a sob. "I tried to run, but the groceries—" Her voice caught, and her lip trembled. Her gaze dropped to me. "No one stopped to help." She shook her head. "He grabbed me. Slapped me." Her fingers touched the welt on her cheek.

"Did he say why?"

"He said I was cheating."

I watched her.

"I haven't."

"It's okay."

"I wouldn't," she pleaded.

"I believe you."

"He doesn't." She rolled her lips into her mouth to stop them from trembling.

"No matter what you say, he never will." I pointed toward the marks on her throat. "What happened?"

"He put his hand there. He said he would kill me if he caught me doing it. I kept telling him I didn't."

"How'd you get away?"

"Some cars were honking, but no one stopped. He could have—" Whatever thought she had caused her to shiver. "When he let go, I dropped my groceries and ran." The tears started then. She threw her hands in the air. "The groceries! Can you believe that? He hit me and choked me, and I held onto those bags like my life depended on them. When I could finally run, I dropped them."

"You were scared."

She wiped at her tears. "I thought he was going to kill me."

"He might have. You need to report what he did."

Rosa shook her head. "I can't."

"He assaulted you and broke the No Contact Order. That's a ticket straight to jail."

"He'll know I called them."

I leaned in. "Rosa, he's never going to stop. If you don't report this, he'll know that you're afraid. Next time won't be a slap or a choke; it will be worse. Guys like him don't deescalate."

"But he'll get madder."

"He assaulted you. He violated the law. That's a felony. The cops need to know so they can find him and arrest him."

My words sounded hypocritical in my ears because of the acts I'd recently committed. Were my felonious actions justified because they were in the pursuit of justice? I hoped so.

"But he went to jail on Saturday," she said, "and a judge let him out on Monday morning. Jail doesn't scare him." She sighed. "What's a couple more days to him?"

"You have to call." I moved for my phone but remembered that I'd lost it. "Let's go to your apartment. I'll go with you."

Reluctantly, she stood. "I don't know why it has to be this way."

"Because he has the order. You have to report when he does something."

"No. I mean, every time I get a guy, it turns into some mess." She wiped away more tears. "Love's hard."

"That isn't love," I said.

***

After the cops left Rosa's apartment, I returned to my unit and tried to get a little extra sleep. The apartment was stuffy, and the box fan loudly whirred as it tried to push the warm air outside.

As I lay in bed, images from the last few days bounced around in my head.

Peyton sitting in my apartment telling me about the death of his family.

Detective Ackerman taking me to identify Peyton's body.

Being chased through a north Spokane neighborhood by redneck drug dealers.

Beating Cliff Coffey in the bar to get information.

The drug deal gone bad that resulted in the death of two men.

Committing a burglary and narrowly escaping a confrontation.

After all that, I now had a Spokane Valley address and a possible alias—Joseph Benzo—thanks to an envelope found in a trash can.

For what felt like several minutes, I pondered the idea of giving the envelope to Detective Ackerman. But that would mean admitting to the burglary and some of the other things I'd done.

I let that final thought linger for a moment until I conceded it was a lie.

Oh, I'd committed the crimes, but I wouldn't have to admit to anything. If I gave the Joseph Benzo name and address to Ackerman, the detective wouldn't care how I came into its possession. It wasn't likely to be a procedural issue. Ackerman could simply birddog the name. If it turned out to be Wayne Sadler, he could arrest the man, and the whole affair would be over.

But I wanted to find the fugitive.

It was personal, and that was the truth.

With my decision made, sleep came again.

Chapter 28

Around three in the afternoon, I drove east to Spokane Valley. The brown and tan house was the third lot in from the corner of Twenty-Sixth Avenue and Evergreen Road. A red Jeep Wrangler sat in the double-wide driveway. The garage door was open, but no cars were inside.

I circled the block then parked a house away. For several minutes, I stayed in my truck and tried to determine a course of action.

What if Wayne Sadler was inside the house? I'd seen him earlier in a white Ford Mustang. That car wasn't there now. However, some people have two cars. Maybe he'd loaned out the little sports car, and the Jeep belonged to him.

If the man were there, I thought, he wouldn't know me. We never had contact. His associates—Cliff Coffey, One Tooth, Twitchy, and Scarface had seen me, so the best he would have was a description. Perhaps, Sadler would be suspicious of any stranger approaching him now.

Maybe Sadler had packed up and fled the area. If Joseph Benzo was indeed an alias for Sadler and Patrick Donnelly was his son, then a family connection might keep the man around.

I could have sat in the truck for hours and played a game of what-if. With a final glance around, I slipped out of the vehicle and headed for the house. The small concrete porch didn't leave much opportunity to step away from the door. If Sadler wasn't at this home, I didn't want to scare anyone else by acting suspiciously and moving away from the door after I knocked. To an unsuspecting citizen, there's a fine line between cautious and distrustful behavior.

"Just a moment," a woman called from inside. Footsteps quickly approached. The door opened, and a woman's face appeared. The rest of her hid behind the partially opened door. "Yes?"

"Hi, I'm John Cutler."

I stuck my hand out for her to shake, but she stared at it.

"May I ask you a couple of questions?"

"About?"

"Patrick and Joseph."

Her face flattened. "What about them?"

"Are you Patrick's mother?"

The door closed slightly as she glanced back into the house. "What's this about?"

I removed the envelope from my back pocket then pulled out the picture of Wayne Sadler, Cliff Coffey, and the boy. Pointing to Sadler, I asked, "Is this Joseph Benzo?"

"Unless you tell me what this is about, I'm shutting the door."

"If this man is Patrick's father," I said, "you and your son may be in danger. The police want him."

Her eyes flicked to the picture. "Why? What did he do?"

"Vehicular homicide and fleeing from prosecution."

Her face pinched, and the door opened somewhat. She didn't say anything, though. Her gaze remained firmly locked onto the photograph.

I said, "He's been a fugitive for fifteen years."

"You're lying." She shook her head. "I don't believe you."

"Let me show you something else." I pulled the wanted flyer from the envelope and handed it to her. "His name is not Joe Benzo."

She took the paper with a single hand. "Wayne Sadler?"

"Yes, ma'am."

The wanted flyer shook in her hands. "I don't understand. Joe said he was named after his father."

"He also has another name. Another alias, I mean. Mitchell Pierce."

Her eyes returned to me.

"Have you ever heard that name?"

The woman pushed the paper back to me. "You're lying. Whatever this is, I want you to stop."

"Can I come in?"

"No. Please leave."

"Ma'am, if you won't talk with me, I'll call the police, and they'll come out to talk with you." I took the flyer from her. "They will not leave, and they won't be as nice as I am. They'll ask why you harbored a fugitive."

"I never harbored anyone. He never lived here."

"Helping him—keeping his secret—is rendering criminal assistance. That's a crime."

Her face revealed the fear. "I didn't know."

"Ignorance of the law isn't a defense." This wasn't strictly true, but I was betting she'd heard the adage before without understanding the nuances of it.

Her face reddened as she pulled the door open. "But I didn't know. I swear." She sounded as if something had clicked inside her, and she had gone into an automatic mode. "Come in." The woman turned and walked away.

I stepped into the house and closed the door behind me. The living room was clean, and a large television occupied a corner of the room. A video game system rested in front of the console, and a stereo stood in the opposite corner. Against one wall sat a tan leather couch, and two dark brown recliners took up posts on opposite ends of the room

I reintroduced myself and stuck out my hand again. This time she took it, albeit tentatively.

She was several inches shorter than me. A denim button-up shirt hung outside tan-colored pants. She didn't have shoes on, which revealed the chipping paint on her toenails. It appeared she had trouble swallowing as if she were fighting back her emotions. She whispered, "Alicia Donnelly."

"Not Benzo?"

"Joe and I were never married."

A young boy walked out of the hallway wearing no shirt and a pair of black shorts. Alicia said softly, "This is Patrick."

I nodded at the boy. "Hi."

Patrick ignored me and simply watched his mother. "What's wrong?"

"Nothing," she said.

He turned and went back down the hall.

Alicia watched him leave. "He's at that age."

"What age is that?"

"Eleven." She faced me now. Tears welled in her eyes. "What do you want from me, Mr. Cutler?"

"Where is Joe?"

She pulled her shoulders back and thrust her chin forward. Even though her lip trembled, she defiantly said, "I can't."

"Can't or won't?"

"It doesn't matter. He's Patrick's father."

"He's not a good man."

"Are you kidding me?" She wiped at her eyes. "He helped me buy this house a few years back so that Patrick wouldn't have to live in an apartment anymore. I could never have done this by myself. He always pays his child support. Do you know I never took him to court? We just talked about it, and he agreed. From day one, he's paid like clockwork. When it's his turn to take Patrick, he's always on time and never brings him home late. He's never laid a hand on me. Never demanded anything."

The boy had to be why Wayne Sadler stayed in the region all these years. The fact that he had the joy of a family after taking Peyton's away from him burned in my gut.

Alicia continued. "There've been other men in my life, and I've got to tell you, they all come up short. Joe Benzo is a decent man."

"What about the homicide?"

She looked away. "That's a different man. He might be innocent for all I know. You could have faked that flyer."

"You don't believe that, or you wouldn't have invited me in. Something's not right, and you're afraid to face it."

Her lips pursed.

"Whether you admit it or not, Joe Benzo is Wayne Sadler, and Wayne Sadler is wanted for vehicular homicide. Beyond that, the cops want to talk to him about the killing of three other people."

Alicia's face paled, and she dropped onto the couch. I sat on one of the recliners.

"What are you talking about?"

"Wayne killed a man who knew his true identity. Later, he murdered two drug dealers."

"Drugs?"

"He's running marijuana out of Canada."

"No." She held her head in her hands. "He wouldn't risk everything for drugs."

"Alicia, what do you think he does for a living?"

"I don't know," she muttered.

"He's never said?"

She looked up. "He says he helps people."

"And he helped you buy this house?"

"You're really not a cop?"

"I used to be, but not now."

We sat in silence until she softly admitted, "I don't know where he lives."

"You've never picked up Patrick there?"

"He always picks up and drops off Patrick here. That's what he offered, and I agreed to it. I thought he was being accommodating. He said he lived up in Hillyard and was trying to save me the drive."

I wanted to point out how stupid she'd been, but I could see by the look in her eyes that she was already telling herself the same thing.

"The envelope I found was addressed here."

She nodded. "Mostly from Patrick's school and such. He doesn't get any other mail here."

"Who else might know where he lives?"

"I don't know. I'm not a part of his life."

"Do you know who Cliff Coffey is?"

"Should I?"

"Patrick has a room there."

Alicia cocked her head then called down the hall, "Patrick!"

The boy shuffled into the room. He now had on a Seattle Mariners t-shirt and a pair of tennis shoes.

"Who's Cliff?"

Patrick glowered at me. Alicia grabbed his arm and

pulled him to her.

"Who is this person?" she asked.

The boy scowled at his mother. "I'm not telling you shit."

Alicia's eyes widened. "Do not speak to me that way."

Patrick smirked. "What are you going to do about it?"

She slapped him. Even I jumped in surprise.

The boy squealed. "Mom!"

Alicia shook him. "Tell me who this Cliff person is!"

Tears welled in the boy's eyes. "He's my uncle."

"Do you stay with him?"

Patrick rubbed his cheek and nodded.

Alicia faced me but held onto her son. "Who is Cliff?" she asked. "What does he do?"

"He runs dope."

She pulled Patrick to her and grabbed him by both arms. "Have you seen him do anything bad? Have you ever seen your father do anything bad?"

Patrick's eyes widened, and he danced nervously.

"Have you seen drugs?" she asked.

"I don't know."

"What about guns? Have you seen guns?"

The boy looked at me, but Alicia jerked his attention back to her.

"Have you seen guns?" Her voice was slow, and the words were heavy.

Patrick slowly nodded.

"You've seen guns at your dad's house?"

The boy lowered his eyes and nodded a second time.

"Why didn't you tell me?"

"I didn't want to get dad in trouble."

Alicia grabbed her son's face with both of her hands. "Guns are dangerous."

"I know."

"Go to your room."

Patrick sprinted down the hall and slammed his door.

"I'm sorry," she muttered. I wasn't sure if she was talking to the boy or me.

"I didn't mean to cause problems," I said, "but I need to find Joe."

She shrugged. "I didn't know he was doing any of this stuff."

"But you suspected something."

"I don't know. Maybe." She pulled at the tail of her shirt. "I guess I never asked where Joe got his money." She looked around the living room. "I was just happy to have a home of my own. Is that so wrong?"

"No."

"I wondered where he was getting money for support payments. When I asked about his job, he said he did a little of this and a little of that." She air-quoted what Sadler had said. "Once he said he was in between jobs, but he never missed a support payment."

"Did he mention his family?"

Alicia leaned forward. "He said his parents died when he was young. Why? Are his parents still alive? Does Patrick have grandparents?"

"I don't know. Maybe. Fifteen years ago, his parents were alive. They helped him avoid prosecution for the vehicular homicide."

Alicia looked at the wall and studied a picture of her son. "How could Joe do this to us?"

"He's a bad man," I said.

She finally began to cry.

Standing to leave, I said, "Thank you for your time."

Alicia followed me to the door. "What should I do if

Joe shows up?"

"What do you want to do?"

"I don't know."

"You can pretend you don't know any of this and go on with the way things are. He's the father of your child, after all."

"And if I don't want to pretend?"

"Call the police."

She winced. When I was on the front porch, she said, "I wish you had never told me these things."

Before I could respond, she shut the door.

***

I was northbound on Evergreen Road when I saw the Bronco. The Ford kept a comfortable distance behind me. Even so, I could see three occupants in the rig. I couldn't make them out, but I was reasonably sure who was there. When the light changed to green, I continued.

At Seventeenth, I turned into a residential neighborhood and raced for several blocks before turning north again on another street whose name I missed. I slammed the brakes and waited in the middle of the road.

Seconds later, the Bronco careened around the corner. The vehicle nosedived as its brakes locked. The driver spun the wheel to avoid rear-ending me. The Ford ended partially up on the curb.

Glancing over my shoulder, I immediately made out the three of them. One Tooth was behind the wheel, Scarface was in the passenger seat, and Twitchy sat in the middle of the backseat.

I pressed the accelerator, and my truck fishtailed away. In my rearview mirror, I watched the Bronco lurch onto the sidewalk, bounce back into the street, and clip a motorhome parked curbside. After that, the Ford overcorrected and scraped alongside a parked Volkswagen Beetle.

The Bronco turned onto the first side street it came to, and I lost sight of them after that.

I raced in the opposite direction. For more time than was probably necessary, I drove through neighborhoods. When I felt good and safe that there was no way they could have possibly followed me, I headed toward the freeway.

Chapter 29

When I arrived at Club Royale to start my shift, Bosco said, "You look like the shit."

"Can I work the door tonight?"

"Not feeling well?"

"I'd like to avoid another bottle against the head."

He frowned. "Still crying about that? Try living in the winter of my country. That will give you something to cry about."

"You're all heart, Bosco."

"I am all business. That is why I love America."

"Land of the free."

"Home of the brave. Except you, John. You are not so brave."

"And you are not so trim."

He feigned being hurt and patted his stomach. "I am only short for my weight."

Bosco fit right into America.

***

"How's it going?" Erika asked.

"Fine." I handed the licenses back to two college-aged women, took their money, and waved them in. "Normal night."

From inside the club, Nina Sky's "Move Ya Body" thumped into the night. Several women still in line shook and wiggled in time with the rhythm.

Erika put her lips near my ear and whispered, "Want to

get together after?”

“I can’t.”

“Why not?”

I held a hand up to the couple next in line and said, “Hold on a sec.” Turning to Erika, I whispered, “I’m working on that thing, and I need to get some rest.”

“So? I’ll come over, and we’ll rest together.” Without waiting for my protest, she turned and went into the club.

Time with an attractive woman should be something I looked forward to. Wanting to push her away before she could leave me wasn’t healthy—I knew that. So, why did I want to do it?

I waved the next couple forward.

***

The line was steady, and as usual, there was a rush around eleven. That’s when the real club-goers showed up. They started their night when the citizens were on their way home.

I checked the IDs for a bachelorette party of eleven. They were already primed by the time they arrived. Each of them wore a short, shiny skirt along with a white feathery cap. All appeared to have been overserved elsewhere, and the bride-to-be was drunk. If this were a regular bar, they wouldn’t have gotten access. But with a capacity of four hundred and a dance floor that mainly stayed full, over-service was an almost nightly occurrence. If they could walk and talk, Bosco wanted them inside. Once identified as overserved, a staff member would X their left hand with a black magic marker. The women could still sneak drinks with their friends, but if Bosco was ever questioned by law enforcement, he would have plausible deniability that we cut off the patron in question.

As I said, he fit right into America.

The bachelorette crew danced their way into the club to Justin Timberlake's "Rock Your Body." As she went by, the bride-to-be dragged her hand across my face and blew a kiss. A cheer erupted from inside as the women entered. A bachelorette party would undoubtedly turn up the fun on the dance floor. The last woman into the club turned and waved goodbye. I laughed and distractedly motioned to the next person in line.

"Is the owner in?" Croy Bradford puffed his chest. "I wanna get back in this here club, and he needs to—"

With a kick, my stool skittered away. I jumped at the country boy, dragging him to the ground.

Several women in line screamed. A couple of guys yelled, "Fight!"

For a big kid, Bradford was lightning quick. He had to be—he was a college quarterback—but being a football player didn't mean he knew how to fight. We rolled from the sidewalk into the street. I pushed off him, hit him as I did so, then stood. He clambered to his feet.

Bradford held his hands in the guard position. I flicked a jab, and he awkwardly swatted at my hand with both his. I punched him in the gut and doubled him over. He turned his face up toward me, a sheep waiting for the killing blow.

An arm hooked mine at the elbow and jerked me back. "Hey!" I yelled.

A couple of the other bouncers dragged me away.

"That's the guy!" I hollered. "The one that hit me."

Bradford held his gut and moaned. The kid was playing it up. He couldn't be hurt that bad. Linebackers and defensive ends sacked him, for Christ's sake.

Bosco rushed outside. "What is going on?"

I pointed at the country boy. "That's him!" My voice boomed over the music thumping from inside the club. "The one who hit me with the bottle."

The club owner studied my face, then turned to Bradford. "Is this true?"

"That guy attacked me," the country boy said.

Bosco looked toward the crowd, and several people pointed at me. His face softened. He turned back to Bradford. "What did you do to make him mad?"

"I asked to see you."

"Did you hit my man with the beer bottle?"

The country boy eyed the club owner but never said anything.

Bosco pointed toward the end of the block. "You are not welcome here."

"But—"

"Go, or I will take over." He leaned in menacingly. "You will not like the way I fight."

Croy Bradford straightened. "Fuck you, man." He flipped me the bird. "And fuck you, too."

"Yeah, yeah." Bosco waved him along. "Big talk from a little man. Go home."

The country boy headed away, but he continued yelling profanities into the night sky.

Bosco motioned for the other bouncers to release me. "You two go back inside. And put someone else on the door. You—" he jerked his head for me to follow.

We walked down the block in the opposite direction that Croy Bradford had gone. When we were out of earshot of any customers, Bosco said, "This fighting is bad for business."

There was nothing to say. I'd let my temper get the better of me. I shoved my hands in my pockets and prepared for the consequences.

"Bad for business," he repeated. Bosco's eyes measured me. "You should have found someplace away from here and hurt him as he hurt you. Do you understand?"

"Is that the way in your country?"

"It is the American way, too." Bosco shook his head. "What you did is no good. People saw. They talk. People think we are not a safe place to come." He pointed at the line. "Look. Even now some are leaving. Not good." Bosco turned back to me and frowned. "You are a good worker, but this—"

"I'm still a good worker."

He crossed his arms and grunted. "Too many saw what happened. Take off two weeks. No pay. Then you come back."

"This is bullshit."

Dull anger flashed somewhere deep in Bosco's eyes. "Shut your mouth."

Scolded, I averted my eyes. The first thought that came to mind was that I needed this job. I had rent and child support.

"Two weeks," Bosco said. "Then you come back. No more argument."

He walked away then.

I didn't feel like returning to my apartment—partly because I didn't want to be alone but mostly because I was still amped and angry.

There were other things I could do with this energy, though. Other things that would be more productive. Other things that might allow me to burn it off. I could run by the Playground and see if Cliff Coffey was working. If not, I would run out to his house. I wasn't sure what I would do then, but I'd deal with that problem if and when it arose.

As I stuck the key into the door of my pickup, I sensed movement behind me a second before pain erupted in my kidney. It dropped me to a knee. Another blow to my back forced my face into the side of my truck.

The image of my gun sitting on my kitchen counter flashed through my mind. I never took it to work. It was against the law. Besides, Bosco forbade it. He was the only one allowed to have a gun inside the club.

Blows continued to land about my head and shoulders as a thick, velvety blackness pushed in on my reality.

Chapter 30

When I awoke, everything was dark. My hands were bound behind my back, and my ankles were tied together. I moved my head, and a scratchy fabric dragged across my face. A blanket must have been tossed over me. Why would someone do such a thing? Concealment meant I was near where people could see me. I closed my eyes and focused on my other senses.

My mouth wasn't gagged or taped. Whoever abducted me wasn't worried about me hollering for help.

Whatever I lay on rumbled and swayed. An engine protested nearby. I was in a vehicle, but not a trunk. I'd been in a trunk before and whatever I was in now was better. I wasn't fully stretched out, but it felt like I had more room. The blanket, I thought. I was in the back of a big vehicle, and someone covered me up so I couldn't be seen.

There were other engines nearby now. We were in traffic. All of us idling. Were we at a stoplight?

Who did this to me? My first thought was Croy Bradford. I'd just fought the country boy, but he had headed off in the opposite direction. Although, it wasn't inconceivable that he circled the block and jumped me in retribution.

But I was bound and in a moving vehicle. That meant a couple of things. First, the person had a rope. My hands weren't zip-tied or duct-taped. I could feel the rope. Which meant they preplanned this abduction. Second, beating a man is one thing. Lifting him into a rig and hogtying him is something entirely different. That would likely mean the person had help—and they had bad intentions.

So, if it wasn't Bradford, there were only two other people I'd run afoul of recently. Rosa's boyfriend, Houston, didn't seem the type to quietly jump me, then bind my hands and toss me into a vehicle. But there was a person I'd run across who had help.

My body tensed when a male voice said, "He's up." It sounded familiar, but I couldn't assign it.

"How do you know?" Another male. This one was also familiar. I couldn't place it either.

"I saw the blanket move."

"Keep an eye on him," the second voice said.

"I am."

"If he moves, hit him to keep him down, but don't make it obvious. We don't need some looky-loo seeing what we got going on."

"Yeah, yeah."

The engines around us revved. When ours started forward, the vehicle swayed, and the rumbling underneath us returned. I did my best to remain still.

"He move again?" the second voice asked.

"No."

"Maybe," a third male voice said, "it was an optical delusion. A trick of the streetlights."

Even if I couldn't assign their voices, I knew for sure who the three were—Twitchy, Scarface, and One Tooth.

The third voice said, "Or he's playing possum. Hit him just to make sure."

Blows rained down. I did my best not to cry out, but I wanted to scream with rage. Doing so would only continue the assault. The man hitting me gasped as he continued his work. When he ran out of gas, he said through gasps, "If he wasn't… out before… he's out now."

"Good work." The second voice again. "We've got another fifteen minutes to Cliff's place. We'll wake his ass up then and finally get some answers."

***

The vehicle stopped, and three doors opened. The car shifted before the doors closed. When the back door flopped down, I remained still. No good would come from struggling. I was bound at the hands and ankles. They wanted some answers, so they weren't going to kill me right away. My opportunity to escape wasn't now.

Several hands grabbed me and hoisted my body into the air. They jostled me into the house and dropped me onto the floor. Try as I might, I couldn't contain the expel of air when I hit.

"Oof!"

The blanket was ripped away. I lay on the newspaper next to a torn apart motorcycle engine. The lights were on in the house. Someone kicked me in the back, and I jerked from the pain.

"Get up," One Tooth said as he leaned over. White tape covered his nose, and the dark circles surrounded his eyes. They were the aftereffects of our fight. His breath smelled like rancid bacon as he spoke. "Why are you're looking for Mitch?"

"Your mother misses him," I said.

One Tooth punched my temple, sandwiching my head with the floor. Howling in pain, he jumped up and shook his hand. "Shit!" He turned quickly and kicked me in the stomach.

I scrunched as pain cut through my body. My breath

shallowed out, and I struggled for air.

One Tooth bent over me. "Smart off again, and you'll get—"

"Tommy," one of the other guys said.

"*What?*"

"Don't rough him up too much. Mitch wants to talk to him."

Tommy One Tooth sneered. "Guess we need to keep you safe and sound." He slapped my face a couple of times. "How's that make you feel?"

I didn't say anything.

"You're a fast learner," Tommy said and slapped my face a final time. "All of us are gonna wait here until Cliff and Mitch get back. We'll figure out what the plan is, but I gotta say it doesn't look good for you."

The newspaper crinkled as I laid my head on it. After a few minutes, I closed my eyes and feigned sleep. I hoped they wouldn't ask questions I had no intention of answering. I also hoped they would say something stupid if they thought I wasn't listening.

I'll give them some credit, though. They were smart enough to turn on a rock radio station before stepping outside for a private conversation.

As AC/DC sang about the "Highway to Hell," I struggled to get free. The bindings on my wrists were tight, and I couldn't get any play from them. My ankles were also bound, but those ties seemed loose. I frantically wriggled my feet.

During a lull between the song and an advertisement for a local hardware store, I heard the men outside, and I froze. I couldn't understand what they were saying, but their voices were raised. It sounded as if they were arguing. Then the stupid advertisement started, and I couldn't hear them anymore.

"They want to kill you," a soft and afraid voice said.

I flipped over so I could see him. Patrick Donnelly knelt in the middle of the hallway.

"How do you know?"

He hugged himself. "I heard them talking."

"When did you get here?"

"Uncle Cliff brought me earlier."

"Where's Uncle Cliff now?"

Headlights swung over the living room walls. Patrick stood slightly and peered out the window. When he returned to his kneeling position, he said, "He just got back."

"Did Cliff get your dad?"

Patrick shook his head. "He went to the store for some beer."

A door slammed outside, and I craned my head toward the kitchen. A new song started. Tom Petty and the Heartbreaker's "Refugee" muffled the men's voices, and I could no longer hear them.

Looking back to Patrick, I asked, "Is your dad on the way?"

"I think so."

"Can you untie me?"

He squeezed himself tighter. "They'll know."

I continued working my feet back and forth as I spoke with the boy. "You called your father that day I met you."

Patrick nodded, and tears welled in his eyes.

"Did you tell your mom that you called him?"

"Dad told me not to."

Wishing I could hear the voices outside brought a swell of panic inside my chest. "Killing is wrong."

"My dad won't let them do that to you."

"You don't know that."

He started to stand.

"Wait. What if they make him go along? It's four against one, right?"

Patrick settled back to his knees.

"Your dad might want to help me, but he might not have a choice." Saying those words seemed an insult to Peyton's memory but dying here wouldn't help either of us.

The boy seemed to consider my words. He was old enough to understand peer pressure. Slowly, he nodded. "They could say mean things to him."

"Right. So, you need to help me."

"Then Uncle Cliff will be mad, and I'll get in trouble."

"What would your mom want you to do?"

Tears welled in his eyes. He stood but still hugged himself.

"Patrick, *please*."

The boy reached for the ropes around my wrists. "They're too tight."

"Go into the kitchen and get a knife. Don't let them see you."

Patrick ran out of sight. A moment later, he returned with a paring knife. "Will this work?" He seemed proud of his find.

"Start cutting."

The boy sawed on the rope around my wrists as Tom Petty continued to croon. God, how I wished I could hear the four men outside. As the ropes slackened, I yanked a hand loose and took the paring knife from Patrick.

"Go back to your room," I said. "Hide under your bed."

The boy's eyes widened.

"*Please*," I whispered harshly. "Now."

Patrick darted away, and I cut my ankles free. I hurried

into the kitchen, keeping low and away from the windows. Searching for a weapon, I snatched a large knife from a rack on the counter.

Outside, the arguing stopped, but the men's voices could still be heard. Something had been decided. They moved toward the house.

I stepped behind the kitchen door and waited. Their voices were barely audible over the radio. What they said was unclear, but they seemed to be right outside the house.

Could I run out the front door? If I made it, where would I go? If I remembered correctly, the nearest neighbor was several hundred yards away. And it was late. After midnight, for sure. Would a person answer their door out here? And if I ran to the road, the four men would surely find me.

My best bet was to stand my ground.

A song started on the radio I'd never heard. Its chorus, "One Way... Or Another," looped around the small kitchen.

On the nearby table, I noticed my car keys and my wallet. My driver's license was sitting next to them. I shoved them into my pocket. If they didn't already know where I lived, I wasn't worried about them finding it from the ID card; it still showed my previous address in Seattle. I hadn't bothered to update it since moving to Spokane. But they'd found my truck in the club's parking lot. They were close enough to home.

There was a metallic screech from outside then the main door to the house swung inward. Stepping behind the opening door, I heard the men now.

Scarface entered the kitchen first, followed closely by Twitchy.

"All right, already," Tommy One Tooth said from the

other side of the door. "I told you I was sorry."

"What if he had seen what we got going on?" Cliff Coffey asked. I smelled cigarette smoke. He must have stopped just outside.

At the edge of the kitchen now, Scarface stopped. He must have realized I was gone. This caused Twitchy to collide with him. Tommy brought up the rear and almost bumped into them both.

"The hell—?" Twitchy snapped.

"Look," Scarface said, pointing into the living room.

Even though Cliff Coffey was still outside, I couldn't wait. I only had a small window of opportunity, and this was it. I grabbed Tommy by the hair and yanked him. He bleated as he stumbled backward into my chest. I held the knife against his throat.

Scarface and Twitchy whirled around. Both men had guns tucked into the front of their jeans. A couple of heavy metal cowboys. When they reached for them, I said, "Don't," and pressed the knife harder against Tommy's neck.

"Don't!" Tommy One Tooth screamed.

Cliff Coffey burst into the house with a nub of a cigarette between his fingers. He glanced at me, then at his friends. "The fuck?"

"Drop your guns," I said.

Scarface said, "No" and reached for his waistband

Coffey pointed at the man. "Don't you think about it, Brent. He's got Tommy." He turned to me. "Relax, man. Just relax."

"I am relaxed."

He threw the cigarette nub through the opening in the screen door. "There's no way you get out of here alive."

"If I don't live, neither does Tommy."

"Cliff," Tommy begged.

"It's okay, baby brother. I'll get you out of this." Coffey eyed Brent and Twitchy. "You two, drop your guns."

"But—" Brent protested.

"Now!" Coffey barked.

The two men reluctantly removed their guns and laid them on the floor.

"Kick them over," I said.

Halfheartedly, they did so. Neither gun made it to me.

I cast a sideways glance to Coffey. "Now, you."

"What about me?"

"Pull out your gun."

"I don't have—" Coffey lazily lifted his hands in the air. "Hey! Take it easy on my brother. Look at the blood."

"There's *blood*?" Tommy whined.

"There'll be more," I said, "if your brother doesn't put down his gun."

"I don't have one!" Coffey shouted. He lifted his shirt and turned in a full circle. Then he pulled up each pant leg. "I don't do guns."

"He doesn't do guns," Tommy whispered.

Brent and Twitchy shook their heads. The left side of Twitchy's face spasmed wildly.

"Fine." I jerked my head toward the heavy metal cowboys. "Cliff, get over with those two."

Coffey moved toward the edge of the kitchen.

"Will someone please shut off that music?"

Twitchy flicked off the radio, and silence filled the house. When he reappeared, his face continued to tic, and he now blinked uncontrollably.

"Tommy," I said, "put your hands in your front pockets."

Tommy One Tooth tucked his hands into his jeans.

"Where's *your* gun?" I asked.

"In the back of my pants."

I hadn't felt it when he bumped into me, but I wasn't overly concerned about him grabbing it. We were about a foot apart with my hand tangled in his hair and a knife stuck to his throat. Glancing down, I saw the butt of a revolver peeking out from the back of his jeans.

Now, I had a quandary. There were four men—three of which were unarmed. If I were to let go of Tommy's hair to grab the gun, the man could jump away, the others could grab their weapons, and I would be in a world of hurt.

If I moved the knife away from Tommy's throat to grab the gun, he could turn and fight. It might be difficult with my hand in his hair, but it wasn't impossible. And that small break in time would allow the others to retrieve their guns. Again, I would be in trouble.

My options were limited.

"You three," I said and lifted my chin, "stay where you are. Tommy and I are going outside."

"The hell you are," Cliff said.

Tommy cried, "Don't let him kill me!"

Scarface and Twitchy inched forward.

"Everybody relax," I said. "I don't want to kill Tommy any more than you want me to."

The three of them glanced among each other. They hadn't formulated a plan yet, so I still had time.

"Tommy," I said, "Do what I say, and we'll both live to see tomorrow."

"Yeah, man, whatever you say."

"Do you have your car keys?"

"Uh-huh."

"Then let's go."

With my hand clamped onto his hair and the knife

pressed firmly against his throat, Tommy and I shuffled around the kitchen door and onto the back porch. If my hostage wanted to make a play, this would be the spot.

When we made it to the ground, I told Tommy to "call the others out" as much to get them to follow us as to keep his mind busy.

"Hey, guys!" Tommy hollered. "Come out here."

"No guns," I said.

"Leave the guns!" he shouted. "Don't do anything stupid."

So far, he was a fantastic hostage.

Cliff, Brent, and Twitchy exited the house and stood in a line like chastised children. Tommy and I backpedaled around the house under the lean-to. The others followed us.

"You won't get away with this," Cliff said.

"We found you before," Brent added.

Twitchy got into the act. "We know where you work."

Both Brent and Cliff hit him in opposite arms.

"What did I say?" Twitchy griped. "You guys were saying stuff."

From over Tommy's shoulder, I said, "You three—on the ground."

Twitchy looked at Brent before lying down. Cliff reluctantly followed him. Brent remained standing.

"You too," I said.

"I owe you."

"I'm sure."

"Next time won't go like this."

"There won't be a next time," I said.

Brent smiled. "Oh, there'll be a next time. Trust me on that." Then he slowly lay on the ground.

I stepped around the Bronco to the rusty Chevy Luv

pickup. "On your knees, Tommy."

"Oh, Jesus," Tommy whispered. His voice wavered. "You don't have to do this."

When he knelt, I pressed his head into the truck. I removed the knife from his throat and stabbed the right front tire. Air hissed as it escaped.

"Hey!" Cliff shouted. "What are you doing over there?"

"Shut up!" Tommy and I hollered together.

"Now the rear," I said.

"Yeah, okay, man. I get it. I'm cool with what—"

He knelt, and I smashed his head against the truck.

"Nuh."

I jammed the knife into the rear tire, and it snapped at the hilt.

Tommy tensed. "What was that?"

I tugged the revolver from Tommy's waistband.

"Gimme the keys," I said.

Tommy One Tooth reached into a pocket and came out with a set of keys attached to a purple rabbit's foot.

With the gun pressed into his back, I walked Tommy back around the Bronco.

"Lie down with your friends," I said with a push.

He stumbled forward, and the others started a chatter of threats. I waved Tommy's gun at them. That brought some quiet.

When Tommy lay on the ground, I climbed into the Bronco. It fired up, and I dropped it into reverse. The tires spun on the gravel before it sped out of the driveway. The Ford whipped backward onto Dunlop Road.

I sped away from Cliff Coffey's home.

***

I drove back to the city as if I were a spy in a foreign country—continually checking my rearview mirror, occasionally making unexpected turns, and even once doubling back—all in hopes of eluding or at least identifying someone tailing me.

No one was.

Eventually, I stopped at a convenience store on Division Street and found a payphone. They were getting harder to find. How much longer would it be before they vanished altogether? I wiped the sweat from my forehead as the phone rang.

When the operator answered, I asked to speak with Detective Ackerman. The male operator politely explained that I had called the wrong number.

"Nine-one-one is for emergencies, sir," he said. "Not for delivering messages."

He then gave me the front desk's number. I hung up and called there only to be informed by a recording that the police department's information booth was open from eight to five, Monday through Friday.

I redialed 911 again and got another operator. I informed her that I just called but couldn't get Detective Ackerman through the front desk line. She sternly told me that I was calling an emergency line.

"If you would like," she said, "I can have a couple of patrol officers come to your location and explain the difference between emergencies and non-emergencies."

I hung up.

If I had wanted to talk with the uniform officers, I would have. I had been kidnapped and assaulted. But they would have sent county deputies because the incident occurred in Deer Park. No, that's not true. They grabbed me downtown, so it would have been a city response that would require county involvement. Multijurisdictional, they would deem it. Yeah, that's what I wanted to deal with at that hour.

And what would the story be? I assaulted Cliff then forced him into his bar, where I assaulted him some more. Maybe the boys had proof I burglarized Cliff's house. Who knew? And so, yeah, they committed a felony by grabbing me and taking me to Cliff's house, but I assaulted Tommy with a deadly weapon. I held him against his will. Committed malicious mischief by slashing the tires then stole a vehicle to escape.

Trying to explain my innocence to a bunch of unsympathetic uniforms didn't seem like the best use of my time. I could report all of this later to Ackerman.

And what if the *Deliverance* boys called the police? There's no accounting for the actions of some people. The last thing I wanted was to be caught in a stolen Bronco. I threw the Ford's keys into the street.

The walk back to my apartment was only a couple of miles.

I would call Ackerman in the morning and update him. Until then, I would lay low. I had Wayne Sadler's attention. I was supposed to be chasing him, not the other way around.

Chapter 31

Around two-thirty in the morning, there was a light tapping at my door. I wasn't worried about it being Wayne Sadler or his boys—they wouldn't knock so nicely—but that didn't stop me from asking, "Who is it?"

"It's Erika," she whispered. "Who else would it be?"

When I opened the door, she stepped in. "Boy, you sure caused a stir tonight."

Corporal came over and diverted Erika's attention by sticking his head into her belly. She ruffled his ears and cooed as if talking to a baby. She said he was a good boy or some other nonsense. I could barely understand her baby talk, but the dog seemed to like it. His tail wagged, and he panted heavily. When she looked up, Erika's smile faded. "You look like hell."

I'd gotten home an hour ago and showered after walking Corporal. My entire body was sore. When they grabbed me, Sadler's boys hit me about the back, shoulders, and head. Then while in the car, one of them—I'm pretty sure it was Twitchy—beat me while I remained covered with a blanket.

This was after the brief fight I had with Croy Bradford outside the club. Brawling isn't like the movies. Even a quick bout leaves the winner with aches and pains.

I said, "Some guys tried to bust me open like a piñata."

She cringed but continued petting the dog. "That's horrible. They hit you with sticks?"

"What? No. It's a metaphor."

"They didn't hang you in the air, then? Because, if they did—"

"They beat me was all."

"Oh, so, like a drum."

I frowned.

"Less dramatic, but more accurate." She turned to the dog and tutted. "Isn't that right, big boy? Less dwa-matic and more acc-u-what." I understood her words that time. Corporal wagged his tail in agreement.

Without looking up, Erika asked, "Was Croy part of it?"

"No."

She straightened and pushed the dog away. Corporal found a spot to lay and watch us. "Are you mad at me?"

"For the dramatic comment?"

Erika shook her head. "No. About Croy hitting you with the bottle. Maybe you should have told the cops about it. My brother made a bad decision to help him."

"Has Isaiah come around yet?"

"He doesn't think he did anything wrong."

"Huh."

"Yeah. He doesn't think I helped him, either."

"Wanna bet?"

"That's what I tried to tell him."

"You're the reason Croy wasn't arrested for the assault, and Isaiah didn't get arrested for some sort of rendering aid charge."

She gently cradled my face in her hands. "Did you get fired tonight? That's the rumor."

"Bosco said to take a couple weeks off."

"A vacation then."

"That's one way to look at it."

She pulled my head down and kissed my forehead, my nose, and then my lips. When we broke, she stepped back and grabbed the bottom of her shirt.

"Erika," I said. "You don't owe me anything."

"Who said I'm doing this for you?"

***

In the morning, I found Erika on the couch flipping through a *Sports Illustrated*. The only thing she wore was one of my plain black t-shirts.

"Good morning, sleepyhead." She tossed the magazine onto the couch. "Want me to make some breakfast?"

"Just coffee."

"It's going. Let me know if you want something to eat. I'm happy to make it."

She was too chipper for this time of day. I poured a cup of coffee.

"I work tonight," she said, "but that leaves the whole day to play. Want to do something?"

I sat next to her and sipped the coffee. "I can't. I'm working that thing."

"You can't take a day off? You could use a break from being a drum."

"A piñata," I corrected. "Besides, his guys came after me last night. That means he's getting scared. I don't want to lose the momentum."

"If that's true, shouldn't you call the cops? Let them take over now."

It was an honest question and one I grappled with during the night. The smart choice was to call Detective Ackerman and let him handle the problem. That's what I had initially planned to do at the beginning of my walk the previous evening. But Sadler's crew made it personal by kidnapping me.

If I wanted to be honest with myself, I made it personal by getting involved. My thinking devolved further when I had the childish thought that Wayne Sadler started this mess by killing my friend. A kid pointing at another and yelling, "He started it," still gets in trouble for throwing a punch in a fight. There wasn't much defense for my actions except that I wanted to be the guy to catch Wayne Sadler.

Old West justice. *Dirty Harry* vengeance. Whatever it was called, I could get in trouble for it. Or worse.

Erika crawled onto my lap and broke my thoughts. I put down my coffee cup.

"What if," she said, "we climb back in bed for an hour? Then you go your way, and I'll go mine."

I snaked my hands around her waist. "If you insist."

She smirked. "Like I have to insist."

Chapter 32

After a shower and a walk over to the park to let the dog run for a few minutes, I headed to Eight Ball Billiards. My gun was under my shirt. I wasn't going anywhere now without some protection.

I once more considered calling Detective Ackerman but decided it could wait. The errand I needed to attend to was more important due to the previous night's events. At least, that's what I convinced myself to believe. It didn't take much effort.

At the pool hall, I found Deacon leaning over the side of a table with a cue in his hands.

A black teenager stood behind him. A pool cue was strung across his shoulders with both hands hanging over either end. He wore baggy jeans and a loose shirt.

Deacon drew his cue back, then gently stroked it forward. The cue ball collided with the last striped ball remaining. It rolled toward the side pocket, where it banged into the pointed edge of the rail and bounced away. Deacon straightened and frowned.

"Side titty," the kid said. "The only time that's a bad thing."

I sat on the nearby bench and watched their game.

The kid lined up a shot on a solid and drove it into a pocket with a resounding thunk. There were now three of those balls remaining. The eight ball was tucked against a side rail.

"Last chance," the kid said. "Double or nothing?"

The fat man smiled. "I already feel bad taking your allowance."

"Allowance?" the kid muttered just before tapping in another ball. "Do I look like I'm on the family dole? I get money hustling fools like you."

Deacon chuckled. "So, this is the long con?"

The kid bent over the table, lined up another shot, and snapped the cue. A ball slapped into a pocket with a satisfying pop. "I've been working you for a couple years now. You just don't know it. Even me letting you in on the con is part of the con."

"Impressive." Deacon winked at me.

The kid's last shot was a tough one. Across the table with a bank. He tapped the nearest pocket with his cue. "One rail." He drew the stick back, eased it forward, and sent the white ball across the felt. The red ball bounced off the rail and traveled back across the green. Before it made it to the pocket, it tapped a side rail and missed the pocket.

Using his cue as a cane, Deacon stood and clapped a hand on the kid's shoulder. "You almost got me."

The look of loss hung on the teenager's face. He dropped onto the bench next to me.

"You still have a chance," I said.

The kid eyed me with suspicion. "He already gave me my chance. It's over."

With two strokes of his pool cue, Deacon sunk the fourteen, then the eight. The fat man and the teenager shook hands as equals. The kid untwisted his cue, stored it in a small case, and left.

Deacon walked over and eased onto the bench. "That's Tremaine."

"Seems like a good player."

"More potential than that, but he's running with a crew.

Time will tell how things go."

"How long have you known him?"

"Long time. I know his mom. Wonderful woman. Tremaine and I have played since he was knee-high. She allows him to come down because of me. The bartenders look the other way. Technically, he's not supposed to be in here." Deacon eyed me with a sideways glance. "But you didn't come by to talk about my protege."

"I need a favor."

"A favor?"

"You can think of it as a favor to Peyton as well."

He squinted. "A favor to a dead friend."

"Have you ever met his dog?"

"Corporal? He brought him around once."

"You like dogs?"

"Not enough to own one."

I looked away.

"What are you asking, Mr. Cutler?"

"If anything happens to me, I need someone to take care of his dog."

"Is something about to happen to you?"

"Maybe."

"I don't want a dog, but that's a good dog, a smart dog. I'll find someone to take care of him."

"Someone nice?"

Deacon shrugged. "Nice, I don't know. But it would be someone Peyton would approve of."

"I'm going to leave a note in my apartment. Who should I say?"

"Use the number for the bar here. Put Deacon. They'll know who."

"You know how the dog was trained?"

He nodded. "The military commands. Peyton explained

some. He should have mixed them up so someone couldn't use them against the dog. Any military man will know them."

"Peyton wasn't paranoid."

"Maybe he should have been." Deacon winced. "I'm sorry. That was uncalled for."

I made a dismissive gesture.

"What's this about?"

"The man I'm chasing knows I'm after him now. His boys grabbed me last night. They gave me a message."

Deacon waggled his pool cue. "But you're going to keep pressing? Maybe you should let someone else find him. Someone who gets paid to risk their lives."

"I've already heard that suggestion."

"And yet you choose to ignore it."

I stood and stuck out my hand. Deacon shook it.

"I'm hardheaded," I said.

***

Back at the Claremont, I stopped by the manager's office and requested some paper and a couple of envelopes. Helen didn't even ask what I wanted them for. I rarely bothered her for such things, so she must have figured it was necessary. She collected the items and handed them to me.

"Do you need stamps?"

"No," I said. "It's not that kind of letter."

She cocked her head and flashed a look of puzzlement.

"Should I be worried?"

I knew what she was suggesting. "It's not that kind of letter, either."

I glanced back once to catch her watching me walk down the hall.

The first note I composed detailed what to do with the dog. It didn't take long to essentially write, call Eight Ball Billiards, and ask for some guy named Deacon. I added a description of him and that he played pool. What more did I know? Not much. I tucked the letter into an envelope and wrote on the front *In Case of Emergency—Instructions for Dog*. Then I put it on the coffee table so even the most obtuse cop could find it.

Then I wrote another letter to my daughter. I'd recently sent her one, but that was the normal "I hope things are going well" sort of nonsense we send in our lives. This letter seemed as if it might need to be more critical.

My first draft seemed too gloomy. I didn't mean for it to be. I intended to tell Erin how much I loved her and how proud I was of the young woman she was growing into. But the letter devolved into incoherent rambling that said I was sorry and that I wished I'd been more involved in her life.

If that were true, why had I spent the last two years in self-imposed exile when I could have lived nearer to her? Isn't that what she would think if she read the letter? In a moment of self-pity, I felt that Wayne Sadler might have been a better father than me. That angered me, and I tore up that draft of the letter.

The next attempt was short and straightforward. I wrote that I was proud of her and was sure she would be a fine woman someday. I added that if anything were to ever happen to me, she should know that I always loved her. After folding the paper, I put it into a letter, addressed it, and put it on the table next to the other.

The dog and I went to the park after that. The summer sun baked the city.

As we walked, my gaze drifted constantly. I was on the lookout for Rosa's boyfriend or Wayne Sadler's boys.

After arriving at the park, the dog did his business near a shrub. When he finished, we turned to leave.

A woman unabashedly yelled, "Hey! You pick that up!"

I eyed the mess Corporal left. "I forgot a pick-up bag."

Her lip curled. "Likely story."

She didn't even know me, but she had me pegged.

***

I still had a few hours to kill, so I sat in my apartment and read a few pages of *The Big Sleep*. I could have gone immediately, but the darkness seemed to be an ally. The dog panted on the floor, and the fan whirred as it struggled to pull the hot, stale air from my apartment.

Waiting wasn't a skill I was particularly good at. There weren't many opportunities to practice hours-long surveillance while a patrol officer. Most times that I sat off a house, a car, or a drug deal were for short periods with the expectation that something would jump off at any moment.

The occasional times when I was posted as security at a homicide scene or such thing, I simply counted minutes. It was an opportunity to get caught up on paperwork, listen to music, or let my mind wander on what else I might enjoy doing rather than what I was doing in that moment. There wasn't something at the end of that task waiting for me to get up and do, so I didn't necessarily feel antsy.

Unlike now.

I planned to go back to Cliff Coffey's house. My first time there was to find Wayne Sadler. I was in a hurry and unprepared. The second time was as a hogtied guest. While in the kitchen in the middle of my escape, I overheard Coffey ask his brother, "What if he had seen what we got going on?"

There wasn't the time or opportunity to follow up on what he meant. Now, I wanted to know. Maybe it could lead to Wayne Sadler.

I tossed my book on the table, and the dog lifted his head. He eyed me for a moment and stopped panting. Then he grunted, returned to panting, and dropped his head back to the floor.

Detective Ackerman, I thought. I should have called him. There was still time. Not only was it smart, but I felt guilty for not doing so already. When I realized that second part, a mirthless smile crossed my lips.

Guilt was a part of life. That's one of my mother's go-to sayings. She raised me with a healthy helping of the stuff. She did it so I wouldn't end up like my father. That was her reasoning, at least.

Your father was a weak man, Johnny.

She loved saying that. Oh, she had plenty of other ones.

Your father was a pig. Don't be like him.

She pulled that one out if I didn't clean my room or burped in public or did any other vulgar things little boys do. She downgraded my father whenever possible.

Not that the guilt and comparisons to my father ever stopped me from doing inappropriate things. I just felt bad while doing them and mentally flogged myself afterward.

Which is what I was doing now—feeling bad about something I hadn't done yet but was going to do anyway.

Is that what my father would have done?

Chapter 33

I drove past the furniture store parking lot. Tommy One Tooth's Bronco was still parked there. The crew either hadn't found it, or they hadn't seen the keys I threw in the street. With a push of the accelerator, I continued north toward Hillyard and the Playground.

When I arrived there, it was almost nine, and the sun was low on the horizon. The little Chevy Luv was parked in the lot. Two odd-sized tires were on the driver's side. One appeared to be a spare. Who knew where the second had come from? The damn thing looked like a jalopy from a cartoon. I couldn't imagine how Cliff Coffey drove the thing.

No other cars in the parking lot looked familiar.

I continued north to Deer Park.

***

I drove by Cliff's house and confirmed no cars were there. After U-turning a quarter mile down the road, I doubled back. This time, I parked on the east side of the house near a clump of trees. It was further away from the arterial and anyone going to Cliff's house would have to consciously look for the pickup at this time of night. I grabbed my gun and exited the truck.

At the rear of the home, I opened the squeaky screen door. Unlike my first visit, the backdoor was closed and locked. It took two kicks to pop open the door. Enough ambient light from the falling sun ensured that I didn't need to flick on any lights. Methodically, I searched every room. Nothing.

"Hell," I muttered and hunted through the house another time.

The second search wasn't any more successful. I stepped outside and checked the area under the lean-to. There seemed to be a bunch of mechanical clutter—an old engine, two flat tires, and an axle were the things I could easily make out. None of it seemed to be something that Cliff Coffey would want me not to see. And besides, I had already walked by all this junk a couple of times.

What was I missing?

I returned to the house and searched for hidden compartments inside closets and cupboards. I was tapping the wall inside Patrick's bedroom when the sound of a small engine caught my attention.

Outside, headlights approached in the driveway. The sun was almost entirely down now.

When the motor stopped, I peeked out the window. It was the Chevy Luv. Cliff Coffey was home.

I waited in the hallway, out of sight from any window in the house.

A thought raced through my mind and sent my heart racing. *The back door!* I had kicked it open and not closed it. Surely, Coffey would see it. Would he still come in if he expected to find his home burglarized? Or would he leave and call Wayne Sadler? Perhaps he would return to his truck and call the cops. There were too many variables to consider.

I stiffened as the screen door's metallic screech pierced the night. There were footsteps in the house now. He hadn't noticed the door was kicked in. Had he forgotten he had closed it?

The kitchen light flicked on, and a shadow was cast into the low light of the living room.

A figure turned the corner and flicked on another light. Twitchy.

He saw me and the gun I pointed at him.

"Uh," he said, and his face exploded with spasms. As I moved toward him, he took a step backward, tripped, and fell onto his butt. His hands immediately went into the air. "I'm sorry!"

Standing over him now, I said, "Roll over and put your hands on your head."

"Why?" More spasms.

I kicked his foot. "On your belly."

He turned over and interlaced his fingers over the back of this head. "Are you going to shoot me?"

"If you make me."

"Man," he said nervously, "I'm not going to make you do anything."

"Do you have a gun? A knife?"

"Huh?"

"Do you—"

"No!" he exclaimed. "I don't have anything."

Starting at his ankles, I frisked him with a single hand. When I got to his waist, I jerked him up and checked his right pocket, then his waist. I did the same to his left side. After I was satisfied that he wasn't carrying a weapon, I stepped back. "Sit up."

He rolled over and sat up with his legs crossed like a kid.

"Did you see my truck?"

"Your truck?"

Parking it on the opposite side of Cliff's house had proved effective at this time of night.

"What's your name?" I asked.

For a second, it seemed like he considered not telling

me, but he muttered, "Mickey."

"What are you doing here, Mickey? This isn't your home."

His face hardened, and he remained silent.

I switched the gun to my left hand. "You were the one who hit me when I was covered with the blanket. Weren't you?"

He smirked. "How could—"

I flicked a jab that caught him unprepared. Mickey flopped backward and brought his hands up to his nose. "Jesus!" he howled through his fingers. "The fuck." He moaned louder when he saw the blood on his hands.

"Sit up."

With reluctance, he did so and kept checking the blood coming from his nose.

"Let's try this again," I said. "What are you doing here?"

"Cliff sent me."

"For?"

"A package."

"What's in the package?"

Mickey's eyes flared, and it seemed he might try to play dumb. I snapped another jab. He flopped back to the floor and rolled to his side. "Stop it!" he cried through the fingers covering his face. "What's your problem?"

"Answer the question."

"Gimme a second."

"You don't need a second. Sit up."

"No." He made the face of a petulant child.

I kicked him in the shin, and he wailed loudly.

"Sit up!

He did so but refused to look at me.

"Is there dope in the package?"

Mickey nodded once. "A buyer is coming to the bar."

"Cliff didn't get fired?"

"For what?" he said through his hands.

"The owner said she was going to fire him."

He checked his fingers for blood again. "Doris says that shit all the time. Every time Cliff does something wrong, she cans his ass. Then he sticks it to her in the kitchen and gets his job back. Lucky bastard."

"And now he's dealing out of the bar?"

"Because of you." His eyes narrowed. "You got Mitch and Cliff all freaked out. We're trying to unload some product and raise some cash."

"There's no dope in the house. I looked."

Mickey's tongue ran over bloody teeth, but he didn't say anything.

"So, where's the dope?"

His eyes flicked to my right hand as it curled into a fist. "Yo, relax, Rocky. It's outside. I'll show you."

"Then why come in here?"

"For the key. It's locked up."

"There's no storage container out there."

Mickey's lips parted into a bloody smile. "That's how we wanted it to look."

I tapped his foot with mine. "Get the key."

He lifted his chin toward the end of the hall. "Can I use the crapper? That's where I was headed when you—"

"The key. Get it."

He frowned and stood. I followed him into the kitchen.

"It's in this drawer," he said.

"If there's a gun or a knife with it, I'm going to shoot you."

His giggle was nervous. "Man, you are one paranoid sumbitch. There's nothing in there but spices and a key.

You can open it if you don't trust me."

"Go ahead." I lifted the gun. "Just remember."

Using a single finger, he pulled the drawer open. "See?"

Inside were tiny bottles with names like thyme, cumin, and turmeric. "Cliff's a pretty good cook," Mickey said. From the drawer, he pulled a white tag with a single key attached to it.

The comment about Cliff's cooking made me think about holidays, which led me to Patrick's room. "Why does Wayne—"

"Who?"

"Mitch," I corrected myself. "Why does Mitch's son have a room here?"

"Mitch used to live here. He still rents the room from Cliff but turned it into a place for his kid. Now, whenever they come out to stay, Mitch sleeps on the couch."

"Where does Mitch live?"

Mickey shrugged. "You think you're paranoid? You got nothing on Mitch. That's a paranoid dude. He's always coming up with new names and different places to stay. What did you call him?"

"Wayne."

"See? There's a new one." Mickey shook his head. "We need a flashlight."

"For?"

"Outside. It's dark." He pointed at a square flashlight on the kitchen counter. "That's what we use."

He led the way, and we walked into the darkness. About fifty yards out, Mickey abruptly stopped. "Here it is."

We were in the middle of a field. The flashlight illuminated the ground. A windbreak of arborvitae trees surrounded the rear of each neighbor's house.

In the distance, a car with a bad muffler raced along the

highway, but I couldn't see its headlights.

Mickey bent at his knees and put the flashlight on the ground. He then brushed dirt, rocks, and other debris away to reveal a small metal door and a padlock. As he slipped the key into the lock, I picked up the flashlight. The movement of light brought a flicker of irritation to his face. It passed quickly, though, and he flipped open the lid.

I pointed the flashlight into the interior of a box built into the ground. A ladder leaned up against the side of one wall. Racks ran the length of the others. The shelves were mostly empty, but some held clear bags containing what appeared to be marijuana. The in-ground shed looked as if it could keep a lot more product.

"How big is the box?" I asked.

"Ten by ten."

"You built it?"

Mickey nodded with the pride of a craftsman. "Me and Tommy. Cool, huh? We wanted to bring power to it, but Cliff said that would defeat the whole purpose of having it. I guess I see his point."

"Is it ever full?"

"Not yet. Right now, we're working on storage capacity. We gotta be ready to make our move. We might be small-time now, but not for long. Mark my words."

With the light, I motioned into the box. "You first."

"You don't want to go down?"

"I'll pass."

"I figured you'd say that." Reluctantly, Mickey climbed into the metal box and looked up.

I pointed the light to a package of dope. "Gimme one of those."

He grabbed a brick and returned to the ladder.

"Just hand it up," I said.

"Huh?"

"Don't climb out."

"Screw that." He put his hands on the ladder. "I'm coming out."

I illuminated the gun in my other hand. It was pointed directly at Mickey.

"When you put it like that." He stepped back from the ladder.

"How many more bricks are down there?"

Mickey turned around, and I gave him some light to count by. "Seventeen."

"Where's the money?"

He looked up. "I'm not telling you that."

Once again, I illuminated the gun. The guy was a slow learner.

"Okay now, relax. I'll tell you. We're parlaying our profits into new shipments. We are only taking out enough to cover expenses. That's why we got the storage capacity. We get a little bigger each time. The plan is to do this for another year or so, and then we'll all retire on some beach."

"Who holds the money until the next parlay?"

"Mitch does, but don't try making me think he's doing something hinky. He's not."

"Why would I do that? It's normal to trust a guy who has a bunch of fake names and changes his address all the time."

Mickey's face twitched.

"Do you know Mitch has been on the run for fifteen years?"

He didn't answer, but the growing spasms on the left side of his face showed the truth.

"His real name is Wayne Sadler. If you ever see him again, ask him about the two women he killed."

His eyes widened. "Huh?"

I flipped the door shut on the box and put my foot on it.

"Hey!" Mickey hollered from inside. The ladder banged against the side of the metal box. "Open up!" He banged on the underside of the lid. "I can't see in here."

I snapped the lock in place.

"Let me out!" Mickey yelled.

I grabbed the brick of marijuana and headed toward the house.

Under the weight of a felony warrant, Wayne Sadler prospered on the habits of weaker men. But there was no telling how much money he sat on. Perhaps it was true that this crew was rolling all their profits into buying more drugs. But a drug deal did not go down at the warehouse as planned. Did that mean Sadler still had those funds squirreled away and had access to them?

Was it fifty thousand? A hundred? Was it so far out to imagine that they had several hundred thousand?

Even a small amount of money represented freedom. It would allow Sadler to pick up and go at a moment's notice. The more money, the further he could run and the easier he could disappear.

Had Sadler already left? The way Mickey talked, it didn't seem the man had, but his window for freedom was closing.

I was lost in thoughts of Wayne Sadler when I heard motorcycles approaching.

***

I lay on the ground at the furthest corner of the house and tried to catch my breath. I'd run there in the darkness with the flashlight turned off. Unfortunately, my foot caught in a hole, and I fell. The brick of marijuana went one way, and the unilluminated flashlight went another. I belly-flopped onto the hard ground, and my jaw slammed violently closed. The ringing in my ears was just starting to ease.

At least, I had enough wits to check for my gun. It remained safely tucked in the back of my jeans.

I crawled to the corner of the house in the hope of watching the motorcycles drive by, but I knew that wasn't going to happen. They were drawing closer now. I couldn't see them from where I lay. By their sound, they were coming up the driveway on the opposite side of Cliff Coffey's house.

The motorcycles didn't have the low throaty roar of the Harley Davidson brand. Instead, they had the rattle and cough of dirt bikes. Like the one torn apart inside the house.

Could it be buyers for the marijuana, and they decided to ride dirt bikes if they had to go off-road. No, I quickly decided. Coffey wouldn't send a buyer here. He seemed more thoughtful than that. If a buyer got the drop on Mickey, they could make off with the crew's entire stash. Coffey wouldn't risk that.

So, who was here now on the noisy bikes? Likely it was some of the crew, but how many would be the question.

It seemed forever before the bikes quieted and the riders entered the house. I was confident that there were at least two from the sound of the engines.

I considered making a run for it. Just sprint around the side of the house and head for my truck. But what if someone remained out front? Then I would have exposed myself without cover or concealment. Yes, it was night, but the moon would illuminate me enough for someone to either get a shot off or to chase me. Either option wasn't one I wanted to explore.

The back door burst open.

"Mickey!" Tommy One Tooth yelled. He clomped down the stairs.

For guys who wanted to keep their operation low-key, they sure brought a lot of attention to themselves with noise.

A muffled voice came from out in the field.

"You hear that?" Tommy said over his shoulder.

"Hear what?" Scarface Brent asked as he now appeared on the back porch.

The muffled voice again.

"That!" Tommy said, and he ran into the darkness.

"I didn't hear nothing," Brent muttered before following his friend deeper into the field.

I crept to the front corner of the house and peered around. Sitting in the driveway were two dirt bikes and Cliff's Chevy Luv.

I sprinted for the road and my pickup.

Chapter 34

While I drove, one decision bothered me—not getting a new cell phone. Not having access to a telephone while chasing a fugitive killer was a bad idea. By itself, chasing a fugitive killer was a terrible concept.

I decided then to contact Detective Ackerman. I should have done it earlier in the day. That had been my plan when I went to see Deacon at Eight Ball Billiards, but I casually ignored it so I could be the hero and find Wayne Sadler myself. Now Ackerman would make me eat humble pie, and I deserved a big helping of the stuff.

Since I was being honest with myself, I should have called him the day before, too. There were plenty of opportunities when I *could* have called but decided against it. And while I was trying to make a truthful examination of my actions, I should have stayed out of the whole damn affair.

But where would things be then?

I liked Ackerman. He seemed like a decent guy, but he wasn't focused solely on finding Wayne Sadler. He had other cases he needed to handle—he was a homicide detective. The guy seemed the type to have a family. He probably went to church. Maybe he was on a softball team. Basically, Gary Ackerman had a life.

If Sadler got caught, I thought, it will be because I made it a priority. I wouldn't let it fall through the cracks.

John Cutler, you selfish bastard, you can justify anything you want.

I rolled my head around my shoulders. My palm banged

gently against the steering wheel as visions popped into my head. Erika in my apartment. The pool game between Deacon and the kid. Corporal racing around the park. Fighting with the country boy, Croy Branford.

Yeah, I thought, finding Peyton's killer was a priority all right. I guess I wasn't as focused on Wayne Sadler as I thought I was. Or I wasn't as attentive as I expected Ackerman to be.

Do as I say, not as I do.

But I had job responsibilities, too. I had rent and bills and a dog that needed tending to.

Justify. Justify. Justify.

"Justify My Love" popped into my head. It was a poppy song from Madonna that still made the occasional rotation in the clubs through a multitude of remixes. Whose love needed justifying?

Erika. I should push her away. I *needed* to push her away. She was a nice girl. She deserved to be with a better guy than me. Because if there was one thing I knew, I'd find a way to hurt or disappoint her, and then she'd leave. Better to be the one to do the pushing than getting pushed.

And here I was, getting distracted again instead of focusing on finding Peyton's killer.

I tapped the steering wheel again to bring my thoughts around to calling Ackerman. What was I going to tell him? What else could I tell him? I had to lay the cards on the table. There was enough dope in Deer Park for Sadler to sell and run off with the proceeds. But he had to split that money four ways. Five, I corrected. I forgot to add him.

But Wayne Sadler still had the money from the drug deal that didn't go down. That's what I suspected, at least. Yet Mickey the Twitch said they needed to raise fast cash. Why?

I could figure all that out later.

No, I corrected. Ackerman could figure that out.

I needed to tell the detective what I discovered and get out of his way. Tell him why I did the things I did and hope he could see my side of things.

My disposition soured as I felt the need to justify my actions again.

Justification was another word for excuses, and I turned over the same garbage Ackerman or another detective would give. We all did the best we could with the time we had. It sounded like a loser's alibi.

I stopped tapping the steering wheel and hit it with a hammer fist. A second and third strike didn't bring me any more satisfaction.

My thoughts jumbled in on themselves after that. They continued to come fast and unorganized, which was how I wanted them because I didn't bother to organize them any better. When I pulled into the Playground's parking lot, I knew why I let the thoughts string out that way. They were another excuse not to stop earlier and use a payphone.

John Cutler, you selfish bastard. My voice.

Your father was a weak man, Johnny. My mother's.

There were a few cars in the parking lot, but no Mustang belonging to Wayne Sadler. Cliff Coffey's truck was at his house courtesy of Mickey the Twitch. My little reasoning meant that Coffey was still inside the building, and now he had nowhere to run. I could go inside, grab the man, and he would take me to wherever Wayne Sadler was hiding.

As soon as I jumped from my truck, I realized the hole in my plan. Just because I didn't have a cell phone didn't mean the boys up in Deer Park were without means of communication. I knew Mickey didn't have a cell phone because I had frisked him and locked him in the box. But Tommy One Tooth or Scarface Brent could, which meant they might have called Coffey or Sadler. There was a phone inside the house, too. Anyone of the boys could have gone inside and called for help.

Blue Öyster Cult's "Burning for You" drifted through the open door of the Playground. The bar owner, Doris, leaned her shoulders against the outside wall as she smoked a cigarette.

"Might as well turn around," she said. She flicked the ash from her cigarette. "He ain't here."

"Where did he go?"

"Hell, if I know. He got a call and left about twenty minutes ago."

About the time it would take for me to get from Deer Park to here, I thought. "Did he get into a car?"

"He walked off into that field." She pointed east into the night. "I asked that fool where he was headed, and he told me to mind my fucking business. I told him that was it—he was fired. Don't bother coming back."

"I thought you already fired him."

Doris studied her cigarette. "Well, about that. We had a conversation, you see." A slight smile played across her lips, but she kept her eyes down. "He reminded me of all the good work he does. *Did.* So, I gave him a second chance." The grin vanished when she looked up, and her gaze hardened. "No more. Not after tonight. I've had enough of his crap."

I pointed inside the bar. "Mind if I use your phone? I need to make a call."

"Gimme a minute to finish this." She held up her cigarette. "I'm on a break, and if I go back in there, I gotta refill drinks. This is the only quiet time I get to myself."

I glanced around the parking lot. A new song drifted from inside the bar. It was one I'd never heard before, but it had the unmistakable sound of classic rock—bluesy guitar, heavy drums, and a thumping bass line.

"Although," Doris said as she contemplated her cigarette, "maybe I should go back inside while I still got the chance. Our days are numbered."

The state wanted to make smoking illegal inside bars. A ballot would go out in November. Bosco and several of the downtown clubs had rallied together to fight it. They were doomed, though. The do-gooders were out to save us all from ourselves. They did it with seatbelts and helmets, and now they wanted to make smokers a pariah amongst society. Once an element realized they could convince the public to vote against their freedoms, liberty was doomed.

I pulled out a crumpled pack of Marlboro's and shook one free. "Let's go inside, and we'll toast the death of independence."

Her smile was crooked. "You're not as bad as Cliff said you were."

***

Had I expected Detective Ackerman to be the first to arrive, I would have been sorely disappointed. A marked patrol unit crept into the parking lot and stopped. Its spotlight turned and illuminated me as I sat on my truck's tailgate. I lifted a hand to shield my eyes.

"You the one who called?" An officer appeared off to my left. He appeared to be in his mid-thirties with a clean-shaven head. Light from the parking lot lights glimmered off his pale skin. He stood bladed to the side with his gun turned away. His hand hovered over the weapon.

I hadn't seen him approach. It was a neat trick—get me focused on the irritating spotlight and sneak through the outer halo of darkness.

Lowering my hand blinded me, so I kept it up and canted my head away. "Yeah, I called. Is Ackerman on the way?"

The officer's eyes flicked left and right, probably checking if there were others with me. The microphone attached to his shoulder crackled with a brief transmission. He reached up with his left hand and covered it. "You told dispatch you were kidnapped."

"That's right."

"Are you hurt?"

"I'm fine. Is Ackerman—"

"Where did this supposedly happen?"

Supposedly? I slid off the tailgate to stand, and the cop stepped back to create some distance between the two of us. With the change of his position, I could see his silver name tag. It read *Thornburg.*

"Listen," I said. "I asked the dispatcher to alert Detective Ackerman. They didn't seem too interested, but I said he'd want to be notified."

Another uniform appeared from the darkness and approached Officer Thornburg. I hadn't heard him drive up. Graveyard cops and their silent approaches, I thought. This one was a little heavier, a little taller, and in his late twenties. He wore a baseball cap with the initials SPD. His silver nametag read *Wixom.*

The two officers exchanged glances before Thornburg repeated, "Where did this happen?"

At least he dropped the 'supposedly' this time.

"Deer Park," I said.

"That's county," Wixom muttered with some

annoyance. "Why did they send us?" he asked the other officer.

Thornburg ignored the question and instead remained focused on me. "Why'd you drive here to report it? There must have been plenty of closer places to call from. Unless, of course, this is where you get your drink on?"

Piqued at the possibility of snagging a DUI arrest, Wixom stepped forward. "Have you been drinking?"

"No," I said. "Not an ounce."

"Uh-huh." Wixom pointed at my truck. "Is this yours?"

"I haven't been drinking."

Wixom's nostrils flared. "I detect the odor of alcohol."

"We're in the parking lot of a bar." It was my turn to point. "The door is open. You can smell the beer from here."

Thornburg tapped Wixom's arm. "Relax."

But the other cop didn't. Wixom leaned in. "Let's have him walk the line."

I waved my hands. "Forget it."

"Forget what?" Thornburg said.

Wixom shook his head. "I'm not forgetting anything."

"Never mind," I said. "I don't want to report anything."

The two exchanged glances again.

"So, now you *weren't* kidnapped?" Thornburg asked.

Wixom's voice took on a menacing tone. "Or was the whole thing some ruse to get us out here?"

"Don't even try the whole false reporting bullshit," I said. My voice rose in self-righteous anger. "I called for help, but this is what I should have expected."

More glances between the two.

I turned to leave, and Wixom grabbed my arm.

"Get off!" I snapped and jerked free.

Wixom shoved me in the back, and my stomach folded

over the tailgate. My hands slapped on the hard metal to stop my face from slamming into it.

"You're not going anywhere." Officer Wixom grabbed my arm and twisted it behind my back. Pain lanced through my shoulder. "Who do you think you are?"

"Let him go." A third voice came from the darkness.

Wixom eased up on my arm, but he leaned his body weight onto me. This pressed my stomach harder onto the edge of the tailgate.

"Hey, Detective," Thornburg said, "this mook was giving us some cockamamie story—"

"Release him," Ackerman ordered.

Wixom surreptitiously twisted my wrist before he pushed off. I spun around, ready to fight.

Ackerman held up a hand. "Easy, John."

"That mother—"

"John!"

I bit off the rest of my expletive.

The detective frowned at Wixom.

"What'd I do?" he asked innocently. "This guy was acting like a drunk. I needed to control him."

Ackerman's gaze shifted to Thornburg.

He said weakly, "His story wasn't making any sense."

"Is that so?" The detective turned to me. "How about it, John? Think you can make some sense now?" Ackerman put his hands on his hips. He looked tired, as if he might have rolled out of bed and hauled ass over to the bar. He wore a fresh pair of Nikes, faded blue jeans, and a Seattle Mariners t-shirt with the late-seventies trident logo.

I said, "Wayne Sadler's guys kidnapped me yesterday."

"Yesterday?" Wixom blurted and threw his hands in the air. Ackerman shot him a sideways glance that cut off any further comment.

"But you escaped?" the detective said.

"That's right. So, I went back out there tonight—"

"Without calling me first?" Ackerman asked.

The question seemed to delight the two uniforms.

"They were trying to keep something secret. They're running dope out of British Columbia."

"You told me that. It's old news."

"But now I know where they're hiding the stuff. They've got seventeen bags of weed hidden in an underground storage unit." I held up my hand to demonstrate the size of the packages.

This changed the demeanor of Thornburg and Wixom. "Shit," they said in unison.

I told them of leaving Mickey in the box, taking a package of weed, and falling in the dark when I heard the approaching motorcycles. That I fled after Tommy and Brent arrived and left the evidence I had taken near the corner of the house.

"So, there might be three guys there now," Ackerman said.

"Five if Cliff Coffey and Wayne Sadler are there. I can show you how to get there."

Ackerman smirked. "Just give me the address."

***

They put together a hasty operation and asked me to wait at a gas station at the southernmost edge of Deer Park. Ackerman contacted the police department's on-shift supervisor who reached out to his cohort at the Spokane County Sheriff's Office. Together, they assembled a team of five officers and deputies along with a county supervisor and Ackerman to check out Cliff Coffey's house.

Another deputy officer was parked near my truck at the gas station lot. She was assigned to keep an eye on me and bring me over after the team contacted the house.

I was on my second cigarette when the deputy exited her car, swirled her arm in the air, then dropped back inside. Her car zipped off into the night. I knew the direction to Coffey's house, but I followed as if losing her might result in extra trouble for myself.

When we arrived at Coffey's place, I pulled off the road behind the deputy. Together, we walked toward Ackerman, who waited alongside Dunlop Road.

He said, "Where's your gun?"

The deputy spun and put her hand on the butt of her weapon. Just that single word changed her demeanor.

"It's in my truck," I said. "Why?"

"There've been some developments." To the deputy, the detective said, "You can go ahead. They need extra help in the back."

She turned and jogged toward the house. Up ahead, the Chevy Luv and two dirt bikes were still parked in the driveway.

Ackerman said, "Tell me again where everyone was when you left."

This wasn't the time for snarky comments. The seriousness on the detective's face showed that something had changed.

"One guy—Mickey—was locked in the underground box."

He didn't lecture me about the unlawful imprisonment or the possibility of the man dying. That alone was a bad sign.

I continued. "When the other guys showed up, I ran

toward the house but dropped the flashlight and dope I was carrying."

Ackerman nodded. "We found them."

"My story checks out."

"Mostly."

I cocked my head.

"Go on."

I pointed at the dirt bikes. "Yeah, so the guys who showed up were Brent and Tommy. I don't know any last names. I'd met them before."

"When they kidnapped you?"

"That's right. Tonight, they checked the house then came outside. They heard Mickey yelling from the storage shed and headed out to him. I didn't stick around after that. My truck was parked over there." I pointed further down the road.

"And you didn't shoot anybody?"

"I did not."

"But you had your gun with you?"

I nodded. "Off the record, I used it to intimidate Mickey to get into the box. You know. Flashed it at him, that sort of thing, but I never fired it. Not once."

Ackerman looked toward the house, and his eyes narrowed.

An engine roared from the east on Dunlop Road. Then a second followed. Their noise reached a crescendo until they slowed as they passed by us. The two patrol cars then pulled into the driveway with their emergency lights rotating.

Neither the detective nor I said anything as deputies exited both vehicles and hurried toward the rear of Cliff Coffey's place.

"That's a big response for weed," I said.

Ackerman smirked. "Weed? You wish."

"I don't understand."

"We found the storage unit, but there wasn't any marijuana in it."

"Then they moved it. You got to believe me. It was there. They probably suspected I would report it."

The detective shook his head. "We didn't find drugs, but we found three bodies. Shot to death. Down in the hole."

Three bodies in the underground box. That meant Cliff Coffey and Wayne Sadler were still out there somewhere. Ackerman watched me with a keen eye.

"Now, wait a minute," I said and tapped my chest. "You don't think I did it?"

"Me? No. But now I've got to jump through the hoops to prove you didn't."

"Which means what?"

"An official interview. I've got to collect your gun for ballistics."

There wasn't any reason to get salty over it. The man was doing it to prove my innocence.

"I should take your truck, too."

"Please don't."

He sighed, then waggled his fingers. "Come on. Let's get the gun. I'm going to end up with an all-nighter because of this goat rope you just gifted me."

Chapter 35

A crime scene technician met us at the police station to conduct a gunshot residue test on my hands. Ackerman introduced her only as "Ann." She was a serious-looking woman in her late forties. She had light skin but almond-shaped eyes and dark hair, which led me to suspect one of her parents were of Asian descent.

Ann opened a small cardboard box that contained seven plastic vials, a shipping envelope, and a pair of latex gloves. After covering her hands, she looked at Ackerman. "Ready."

He motioned toward me.

She opened one of the vials and said, "Left."

I presented my hand, and she daubed along the webbing between the thumb and forefinger. When she finished tapping her path along my hand, Ann closed the vial and slipped it into the white envelope. She repeated the process twice more on the same hand.

She opened the fourth vial and said, "Right." Then she daubed the same path along that hand.

It wasn't an invasive test. I'd seen it done before when I was a patrol officer on the other side of the state but never really understood it. Standing there as Ann tapped along my hand was more tedious than anything.

When she finished with the last vial, Ann closed it and tucked it into the envelope. "Just one more."

"The presumptive test," Ackerman said.

With a cotton strip, Ann swabbed my hand this time instead of daubing. Then she dropped the fabric into a little plastic container. Next, she broke an ampule inside of a dropper and wet the cotton swab. Finally, she secured the plastic container.

Ann looked at Ackerman and said, "All done." She collected the box and envelope before leaving the room.

"So," I said, "did I shoot them or not?"

"The presumptive test takes about five minutes. Ann will let us know when she gets the results. The rest of the kit she'll send to the lab."

"And my gun?"

Ackerman reluctantly shrugged. "It's going to evidence."

"Are you going to collect my clothes, too?"

"It's the right thing to do. Not only do we need to make sure you didn't kill those men, but we need to clear your name of any suspicion."

"Should I strip now?"

"Ann will be back in a few with a change of clothes and photograph what you're wearing."

I crossed my arms.

"Sit down," he said. "Let's start the interview and not waste time. I've already got the tape set up. See that light in the wall? Once it goes red, we're live, and you're being recorded. Understand?"

I nodded.

He pulled out his notebook and removed a Miranda Warning card. "Here we go." He flicked a switch in the wall, and the little light flashed red. He slid the card in front of me so I could follow along. "You have the right to remain silent."

I'd heard them before. Not only had I read them too many times to count, but they'd also been read to me. I'd like to forget those times.

When Ackerman finished reciting my rights from memory, I signed the card and waived my right to an attorney. He started in with his questions. He didn't act as if he were trying to pin anything on me. Instead, his questioning seemed polite. His follow-up queries were thoughtful and only meant to clarify.

About ten minutes into the interview, Ann poked her head back in the small interview room. The detective raised an eyebrow, and she shook her head.

"Thank you," he said. "We'll wrap this up quickly. Can you give me about twenty, and then we'll collect his clothes?"

Ann didn't smile, but the lilt in her voice sounded almost playful. "It's overtime, Detective. Take as long as you want." She closed the door and left.

"The presumptive test came back negative," Ackerman said.

"I told you I didn't shoot anyone."

"It's only presumptive. Gunshot residue is fragile. You might have rubbed it off or washed it off."

"I didn't."

"A defense attorney could intimate that you did, which would cast doubt on their client's guilt. That's why the lab tests will be important, and we'll test your clothes, too."

"My innocence helps proves someone else's guilt?"

"In the eyes of a jury? Maybe."

Ackerman continued with his questions then. I didn't argue about any inquiry and stated facts or what I believed I could assume. The detective was helping to paint a picture of my innocence, and I needed to give him the colors to do so.

At no time during the interview did Ackerman treat me with anything less than respect. The longer the discussion went on, the more shame I felt. Guilt built up inside me until I said, "I'm sorry."

"For?"

"Not calling sooner."

"Might have changed some things."

I knew what he meant—three men might still be alive if I had brought him into the loop earlier.

He let me off the hook by saying, "Then again, maybe it wouldn't have." He closed his notebook. "Let's collect your clothes. Then get you back to your truck."

Ann returned with a camera around her neck. In her hands, she held a set of blue jail pajamas. On top of them were a cheap pair of shower shoes. Ackerman took the clothes and set them on the table. Ann quickly photographed me from four sides—front, back, left, and right—then exited the room.

The detective watched as I slipped out of my clothes.

"Leave them on the table. Ann will step in once you're changed and put them into bags."

I put on the jail pajamas and settled my feet into the shower shoes. God, I hated flip-flops. They left me feeling exposed and weak. Sort of like the pajamas did. Maybe that's why the jail staff dressed their prisoners this way.

Ackerman opened the door and motioned Ann in. Then we left.

***

It was almost three in the morning when I got back to my apartment.

Before that, Detective Ackerman had dropped me off at my truck. Members of the Spokane County Sheriff's Office were still processing the crime scene at Cliff

Coffey's house.

After I unlocked my apartment, I immediately leashed Corporal. The dog had been cooped up most of the day and needed some exercise. I was turning out to be a horrible pet owner.

As we exited the building, Erika trotted up on the sidewalk. She still wore a Club Royale t-shirt. "Hey, you!" She stopped and eyed my outfit. "Were you arrested?"

"Long story."

She fell into step with the dog and me. "Where are you headed?"

"To the park."

"This late? You're brave."

"It's safer than you think, especially with him."

She slid her hand into mine. She didn't ask to tag along. I guess she didn't have to, and I think I didn't mind. Was this how relationships started?

By this hour, most cars were gone from downtown, and only a few people moved about. The city shuts down after the bars close.

"About that story," she prompted. "I want to know how those fancy threads came to be."

Corporal and I guided her to our favorite spot in the park. The lights from the nearby buildings glimmered off the surface of the river. Once unleashed, the dog sprinted into the darkness. Erika and I walked to the water's edge, and I shared the adventures of my night. When I finished my story, she asked, "Were you scared?"

"At times."

A flock of ducks swam toward us. They quacked and chattered as the group paddled in the nearby water.

Erika faced me. "Are you going to keep looking for that guy?"

"I don't know. It's in my blood now, and I want to see the guy caught."

"You sound like those animals that get excited by the thrill of the chase."

I shrugged.

"And you're really not afraid?"

"I didn't say that."

She leaned her head against my shoulder. After a moment, she looked back. "Where'd your dog go?"

"He's around here somewhere."

"I'm ready to go," she whispered.

Turning away from her, I yelled, "Fall in."

Corporal burst out of the bushes and sprinted over. He stopped with his back straight and his mouth closed. I clicked his leash onto his collar and said, "Forward, march."

Erika laughed. "He's an Army dog."

"Almost. He's a Marine dog."

"What's the difference?"

Since I hadn't been in the military, I didn't know how to respond. I settled on, "Different team, same division."

"Well, at least he's trained well."

"I think that's the point."

Chapter 36

I awoke late morning, and Erika was already gone. Either I had been exhausted, or she was stealthy as a ninja. After a shower, I dressed in a pair of blue jeans, a plain gray t-shirt, and a dirty pair of running shoes. My boots were now considered evidence, and I was reasonably sure I wouldn't see them again in this lifetime.

Corporal and I took a spin around the block. He did his usual business in the nearby parking lot. I remembered a plastic bag this time and picked up the mess. Dog owners must love their pets to subject themselves to this type of thing every day.

Could I live with the guilt of pretending not to see it next time?

After locking the dog back in my apartment, I headed west. I needed something, and I didn't know where to get it without going through the appropriate legal process, which meant paperwork and up to a ten-day waiting period for someone to conduct a background check.

But I recently met someone who might be able to direct me where to find what I wanted.

I parked in front of the pool hall. Inside, several tall fans oscillated as they tried to aid the weak central air system, proving itself inadequate at keeping the premises cool. Lynyrd Skynyrd's "Simple Man" drifted through the bar.

Deacon sat alone in his usual corner. He held a glass of ice water to his forehead as he watched me approach. "John Cutler, I might think you want to be friends with how much you keep visiting."

We shook hands, and I sat next to him. Together, we scanned the room's activity.

At the furthest table, a young couple amateurishly slapped the colored balls across the felt. They giggled and fawned over each other whenever a ball dropped from the table.

Next to them, a lone player practiced the same shot over and over. He'd hit a ball, send it across the table to tap another, and watch with patience as the second went into a pocket. Then he would sit two balls back into the positions of the previous ones. Neither was the cue ball, but it didn't matter what he was doing. The shooter would draw back his stick and repeat the process. After each shot, though, his eyes would drift back to Deacon and me.

Two tables were empty before it got to the last table where balls were scattered about.

"Are you in the middle of a game?" I asked.

"Creating the illusion of such."

Same as the lone player honing his skill.

I lowered my volume. "Do you know where I can get a gun?"

Without facing me, he said, "The gun store."

I didn't respond. Instead, I looked down at my hands.

"If you need directions, let me know."

I lifted my head and watched the lone player continue his practice. His eyes flicked in my direction, and it was then I knew he was one of the men from the first time I visited Deacon—one of the men that moved whenever he tapped his pool cue.

"I would have thought," Deacon said, "that an ex-cop would have a gun lying around. Something to be thrown away if a situation so dictated."

"I had one. The cops have it now."

Deacon lowered the glass of ice water from his head and studied me.

"It's considered evidence."

"Are you suspected of something?"

"No, but they collected it nonetheless."

We silently watched the lone player practice as he pretended not to observe us. It was a lesson in street life.

Deacon lifted the cold glass to his neck. "If I help you find a gun," his eyes shifted to mine, "are you planning something illegal with it?"

"It's for protection. I can't wait the ten days."

Silence overtook us once again. I wanted to turn to him and ask him to hurry, but that wasn't the way to do this. I wasn't experienced in this world, yet I knew enough to let things play out in time. If Deacon didn't trust me, I wasn't getting a gun. He would have to get comfortable with the idea.

Several tables away, the lone player continued his practice. He had moved on to working a new shot that allowed him to keep me in sight the entire time.

"Wait here," Deacon muttered. He set his glass on the bench then walked to the payphone. The big man leaned into it and spoke for several minutes.

The lone player stopped practicing and stood with his cue tucked into his shoulder. He no longer attempted to be coy about observing me. I must have missed a signal between Deacon and him. The player's eyes never went elsewhere in the bar. His gaze never drifted to his employer. Instead, they remained impassively on me.

When Deacon finished on the phone, he returned to our bench. As he passed by me, the lone shooter bent over his table and returned to practicing his shot.

"Three hundred," Deacon whispered. "Non-negotiable."

"And it's clean?"

His eyes narrowed as if I'd insulted him. "It will be here in fifteen minutes. If you don't have the cash on you, I suggest you get it fast. If you're not here when the delivery is made, the deal is off. Don't expect another."

Deacon's curtness led me to believe that I had stepped over a line. He held the cold glass back to his sweaty forehead and returned to observing the lone player.

I hurried out of the bar then ran through the city, looking for the nearest ATM. At the Western Bank building, I stepped up to an external machine and slipped in my card. A quick balance check showed that I had barely enough in my savings account.

After sprinting back to the bar, I slowed to a jog as I neared the intersection. Across the street, Tremaine entered the billiard house with a brown paper bag in his hand. The light changed, and I jogged across.

Inside, ZZ Top's "Jesus Just Left Chicago" slid from the speakers.

The lone player stood at the bar with the young couple who'd been playing at the far table. It appeared as if he might be buying them a drink. They seemed happy at the turn of events. The woman shook her hips in time with ZZ Top's bluesy tune.

Now, no one was inside the pool table area except Tremaine and Deacon. The teenager sat alone near the third table. As I passed him, I nodded with a friendly smile, but the kid's face hardened. I continued toward Deacon, but the fat man shook his head once. I stopped and turned around.

On the bench near Tremaine was the paper bag. His

hand was draped over it. I sat next to him with the sack between us.

He looked briefly toward the bar before eyeing me. "Didn't figure you to be in the market for such a thing." For a kid, he didn't seem intimidated by this moment. On the other hand, I felt like everyone in the establishment knew what I was about to do. Maybe they did.

The bills were still in my hand. I set them on the bench and put my hands in my lap. Without looking, Tremaine scooped up the cash, and it disappeared into a pocket.

"You don't know me," he whispered.

Without further word, he stood and left. He didn't bother saying goodbye to Deacon. It was barely perceptible, but Tremaine slipped something to the lone player on his way out.

I collected the bag and moved to where Deacon sat. I peeked inside. It was a snub-nosed revolver. "I should have asked for rounds."

Deacon didn't look at me. His voice remained low. "There are rounds in it. If you want more than that, it's on you."

I stuck my hand out, but he ignored the gesture.

"This is a one-time deal. Come back for business again, and our new friendship will be over."

"I didn't mean to offend."

"Ignorance of the law isn't an excuse. The police say that all the time."

I knew that. I'd already told Alicia Donnelly the same thing.

Deacon continued. "It's the same rules down here. Best know the law before you get yourself in trouble. I helped you because Peyton was a friend, but now you owe me because I owe Tremaine."

"What does that look like?"

He held the glass to his neck. "No idea, but I'm a man that collects favors. Just remember that when I come asking."

I stared at him.

"And I always collect on my debts."

***

Alicia Donnelly cracked open the door, but the security chain stopped it from opening further. "You." Her hair was messy, her eyes were red, and she looked frantic.

"Can I come in?"

"The cops were here."

"I understand."

"They don't know where Joe is." She squinted, and her lips trembled. "Or Wayne or whatever his name is."

She was still coming to terms with the fact that her son's father wasn't Joseph Benzo but rather Wayne Sadler. I tried to break it to her gently when we first met, but it probably became real when the cops showed up.

"He has Patrick," she said.

"Did you tell the police that?"

"Yes." Tears flowed down her face. "What's he going to do?"

"He's going to run, Alicia. And he's probably going to take your son with him."

She closed the door, and I heard the security chain slide. When the door swung open, she said, "He can't do that. He's my son."

"Patrick's his son, too."

"But I don't even know who he is!"

I stepped into the house and walked into the living

room. She looked up and down the street before closing the door. When she turned back to me, she crossed her arms over her chest. "Why are you here?"

"I'm out of ways to find him. Has Joe called you?"

She angrily waved her hand. "Don't call him that. It's a lie. Everything he said was a lie. Call him by his real name. And no, he hasn't called me. He picked up Patrick, and I haven't heard from him again."

"When was this?"

"Friday. He didn't talk to me then. Normally, he comes in and chats me up a bit. Maybe even flirts a little, like maybe we can—" She seemed embarrassed. "Well, he didn't do any of that this time. He just pulled up in that stupid car of his and honked the horn. Patrick yelled goodbye and ran outside. That's the last I heard from him. He was only supposed to have him overnight."

"I saw Patrick."

Alicia latched onto my arms. "Where?"

"Wayne's guys jumped me and took me to Cliff's house. Patrick was there, too. He helped me get away."

She covered her mouth with her hand. "And you left him there?"

"I didn't know he had been taken."

Alicia spun around before dropping heavily onto the couch. She buried her face in her hands. It seemed as if she were about to cry, but she looked up. "He helped you get away?"

"I was tied up, and he cut me loose. He was very brave." That seemed to make her happy.

"How did he look?"

"Fine."

"Did he say anything?"

I thought about telling her that Patrick called his father

during my earlier visit—that this call sent Sadler's boys after me and eventually led to my kidnapping. It also led to Sadler taking his son. But all of that seemed like salt in the wound, so what good would it do? "He didn't say anything," I said.

"Do you think he's okay?"

"I'm sure of it. What did the cops want to know?"

"They asked a bunch of questions. You asked the same kind of things, but I couldn't help them any more than I did you. They said if Wayne called or made any contact to let them know immediately."

"That's what you should do."

She shook her head. "I can't believe I let it get to this point. I trusted him too much."

"He never gave you a reason not to." I had to give her something to hold on to—some excuse to believe that she couldn't have seen this coming.

"Yeah," she muttered. "Never any reason."

"Did the police check Patrick's room?"

She looked up. "What for?"

"Leads to where his father might live."

Alicia stood, and I followed her down the hallway. Inside Patrick's room, the walls were painted in a dual tone. A light gray paint covered the top half, while a bright blue covered the lower portion. Around the room, a thin yellow band was painted between the gray and blue tones. On the wall above the headboard was a sizeable yellow oval with the Batman symbol in the middle.

"Patrick's a fanatic," Alicia said. "The color scheme is from the old-school outfit."

Comic books were stacked on the floor next to his bed, and a couple of Dark Knight posters hung on the wall. Action figures of Batman and his various nemeses were on the small desk in the corner of the room.

"I'm surprised the detective didn't check his room," I said.

"It wasn't a detective," Alicia said. "It was a beat cop. You know? The guys in uniform."

Contacting her would have seemed like something Ackerman would have done himself. Maybe something more pressing had come up, and he sent a patrol officer out.

I slowly went through everything. The desk, the nightstand, and the dresser held the little trinkets young boys hold on to. None of them aided my search for Wayne Sadler.

Taking my time, I rummaged under the bed and in his school bag. His box of toys might have held every Batman figurine imaginable, but nothing helped me find his father.

"Nothing," Alicia said. That single word crushed every hope she held.

I wasn't ready to give up yet. Leaning against the door frame, I studied the room once more. My eyes swept from top to bottom and then did it in reverse. When I found an object that could contain something, I reminded myself of what I already found inside. The final visual sweep didn't reveal anything new.

About to relent, I looked straight up. There was a small shelf above the door. I stepped back into the room and turned around. On the single shelf was a plastic Batman lunch box, a statue of Robin the Boy Wonder, and a Mariners baseball hat.

I grabbed the lunch box and opened it. Inside were various items—candy bars, a Valentine's Day card, and multiple photographs.

Alicia grabbed the Valentine's card and studied it.

"Who is this girl?" she muttered. "He never mentioned liking a girl." She looked at me. "Could he have a girlfriend?"

"What's with the candy?"

Her lip curled. "He's not allowed to have that stuff in the house. He's got cavities." Her attention returned to the card with the big red heart. She waved it. "Why would he hide this?"

It seemed obvious.

"What about these?" I asked and showed her the photographs.

"I don't think I've seen those."

I thumbed through the pictures, handing Alicia each one after looking at it. There were several of Patrick with his father, but all of them were taken inside a home somewhere. Near the bottom of the stack was a photograph of Patrick standing next to Wayne outside a house.

In the background was a light brown rancher with a moderately pitched roof and large front windows. A porch hung from the front of the house, and a garage was attached to the side.

"Is that where he lives?" Alicia asked. "Why wouldn't Patrick show me these pictures?"

"Maybe Wayne asked him not to. You thought he lived up in Hillyard. That's what you said."

She shrugged. "That's what he said. Maybe he was lying about that, too."

I thought about Cliff Coffey walking out of the Playground and into the dark field. Maybe he was headed toward Sadler's house. That would confirm that it was in Hillyard.

Shaking the photograph of Patrick and Wayne outside the house, I asked, "Can I take this with me?"

"If it will help you find my son."

"I'll show it to the detective working the case. He's probably familiar with that part of town, and if he's not, I'm sure he can find one of his officers who has seen it. Can I use your phone?"

She led me into the kitchen and handed me a white cordless telephone. I opened the phone book on the counter. It took a minute, but I finally found the number I wanted.

"Detectives' office," a woman answered. "How may I help you?"

"Detective Ackerman, please."

"I can put you into his voicemail."

"This is important. Can you have him call me?"

"I'm sorry, but—"

"Ma'am," I said, "please. It relates to a homicide he's working."

"Please hold."

A moment later, a male voice came onto the phone. "Lieutenant Dillon."

"Lieutenant, my name is John Cutler, and I'm trying to reach Detective Ackerman."

"I'm sorry, but Detective Ackerman is not going to be available for some time."

"Why? What happened?"

"His car was broadsided early this morning. He's at the hospital right now."

It must have happened after he dropped me off in Deer Park.

"Is he okay?" I asked.

"I can't release any details, but he'll survive. He's going to be sore for some time, though. Give me your name and number. I'll have another detective call you back."

"I'm calling from a friend's house. I won't be here for long."

"Give me your name and address and the case number you're working on."

"I don't have the case number," I said. "It's the murder of Peyton Meyers. My address should be in there."

"Someone will be in touch." He ended the call.

I stared at the phone for a moment then handed it to Alicia.

"What's wrong?" she asked.

"The detective that's chasing Wayne was involved in a collision this morning. He's in the hospital."

"For how long?"

"I don't know."

"Will they assign his cases to another detective?"

"Not if he's expected back soon."

"What do we do?" Alicia asked.

"Go through anything Patrick has or anything you've ever gotten from Wayne. See if you can find an address. If you do, call the police."

"And you? What are you going to do?"

"I'm going to Hillyard." I waggled the picture of Wayne and Patrick standing in front of the light brown rancher. "I'll search every neighborhood if I have to."

Chapter 37

I headed to Hillyard with a starting point in mind—the Playground. Wayne Sadler's white Mustang wasn't in the lot, but I hadn't expected it to be.

Doris, the bar owner, had said Cliff Coffey walked off into the field after getting a phone call. I walked to the edge of the lot and considered her words. In the middle of the open area was a set of train tracks. On the other side was what appeared to be an industrial area. Once there, he could head further east, turn south, or go north.

I was working on the assumption Coffey left the bar to go to Sadler's home, but I had no reason not to believe it. That wasn't true. The boys *had* been at his home. Maybe they *had* called him.

But that didn't seem to make the most sense. If the boys had called Cliff, wouldn't he have tried to sweet talk Doris into borrowing her car?

So, what made them call Sadler instead?

Was it because I stomped on Coffey's phone and broke it?

And one of the dead guys in the box was Tommy One Tooth. That was Cliff's brother. As much as I disliked these guys, I couldn't imagine Coffey driving up to his home to kill his brother. No, someone else did that.

So, Cliff Coffey walked off into the darkness while Wayne Sadler headed north to kill three members of his crew.

***

The industrial neighborhood to the east comprised various building types: concrete tilt-up warehouses, cinderblock shops, and dilapidated houses. The business types that survived in this area were eclectic fare—contractors, specialty repair shops, and occasional artists. A single distribution warehouse for a grocery chain stood like a bully over it all.

It wasn't a big neighborhood. With Freya Street to the west and Havana Street to the east, it was only four double blocks wide. North and south were bordered by Francis and Wellesley Avenues, which seemed about fifteen blocks apart. I lost count, so it might have been a few more than that.

Regardless, I drove every street in this section of town with Patrick Donnelly's photograph tucked into my dashboard. After ninety minutes of driving, I was sure that there was no home resembling the one in the picture.

Could Cliff have walked further south? There were regular neighborhoods in that area. And if he could do that, then he could have easily walked north. I was sure there were homes in the direction.

South seemed to be the best prospect, so I headed in that direction. I crossed Wellesley Avenue and began the same systematic pattern I'd previously done. The diverse nature of buildings continued down into this neighborhood, although more residential homes crept in among industrial buildings.

A pack of dogs ran across the road, and I slammed the brakes. The truck slid in some loose gravel, but the dogs never noticed the danger they faced. They continued along their path of mayhem. I accelerated, and the truck kicked up dust and stones.

Someone once said fortune favors the bold. There's also an old saying about being in the right place at the right time. I'm not sure which quote I should attribute to my luck for checking my rearview mirror when I did. Maybe I only wanted to see if the wild dogs were still around. I'd like to say I'd been checking it regularly while driving just in case I noticed the exact thing I saw, but I hadn't. I'd been so focused on finding the house in the photograph, I never even stopped to consider that a new white Ford might be driving through the neighborhood.

Until it flashed by in my rearview mirror.

For a guy living under the radar, Sadler had chosen his latest car poorly. It was an unmistakable body shape. Ford remade the brand to make the Mustang cool again—Steve McQueen cool. They even used the long-dead actor in its relaunch campaign. Sadler should have picked the previous Mustang model as they were now ubiquitous.

As much as I wanted, I couldn't quickly turn my truck around. I pulled into the parking lot of a lawnmower repair business, reversed into the street, and raced back to where I had seen the Mustang. I turned east.

The white car was gone.

Only a dust cloud from the gravel road remained. I slowed until the haze settled. Dilapidated houses of various makes lined both sides of the streets. Broken down ranchers stood next to rusting mobile homes that resided near prematurely worn-down manufactured homes.

A bunch of kids ran through a dirt yard while another group of children danced through a sprinkler two houses away. Unleashed and collarless dogs roamed free. At one home—a large blue affair with a peeling roof—a Saint Bernard rested on a couch that sat on the front porch.

After three blocks, I stopped in front of a yellow house

that looked vaguely familiar. The house had a nice lawn, a clean yard, and a little white fence. The two-car garage jutted out from the rest of the house. It didn't fit with the neighborhood.

I grabbed the photo from the dashboard and held it up. The house in the picture was brown with tan trim. With that aside, everything else fit—the porch, the size of the windows, and the attached garage were an exact match. Wayne Sadler had painted his home.

A couple of lots up, I pulled to the side of the road and parked. I hurried back to the Sadler house and moved to the garage. Standing on my tiptoes, I saw the Mustang parked inside. Now wasn't the time to be a hero. It was time to call the cops and let them grab a fugitive killer.

As I turned to leave, a young boy yelled from inside the house, "You're not my dad!"

"Get back here," a man hollered.

"I don't have to listen to you."

Around the corner of the house, a screen door opened and slammed. Almost immediately, it happened again. Patrick Donnelly rounded the corner of the house and shouted over his shoulder, "Leave me alone!"

He wasn't paying attention and ran into me. His eyes widened when he looked up. "Whoa."

I grabbed his arm and pulled him behind me.

Cliff Coffey came around the corner. "Patrick, we don't have time—"

He didn't slow his momentum even though he realized too late I wasn't the boy. Dropping my shoulder, I drove into his chest like a linebacker hitting a receiver coming across the middle of the field. Coffey left his feet and desperately reached out for something to break his fall. There was nothing. He landed with a thud.

Patrick peered around me. "Is he okay?"

Coffey lay sprawled on the driveway.

Without looking at the boy, I asked, "Where's your dad?" I needed to keep my eyes on Coffey.

"I don't know."

"Don't tell him nothing," Coffey rasped. He moved now. The surprise of my attack was wearing off. "He wants to hurt your dad."

I put my hand on the boy's back. "Go inside and call nine-one-one. Do you understand?"

The boy hesitated.

"Your mom sent me to find you, Patrick."

"Mom?" He looked up at me.

"She's worried about you. Go call the police. Tell the operator your name."

He turned and ran inside.

Coffey kicked at my leg. It was a stupid and useless move since he was out of kicking distance. The man wasn't a fighter, but we'd already established that fact.

I could pull the gun from the back of my jeans and threaten him, but I was in a neighborhood. There were already witnesses—kids stood around watching us. I was going to have to get information from Coffey with a little subtlety.

"Get up," I said.

He froze. "No."

"The cops are on the way."

"Fuck you."

"Have you heard from your brother?"

Cliff blinked. "Huh?"

"Tommy is your brother, right?"

"Yeah." He dragged the word out for two syllables. "Why?"

"He's dead. Mitch killed him."

Cliff sat up, and it seemed as if he had trouble swallowing.

"Brent and Mickey, too."

"That's why—" He shook his head. "They're not answering their phones. I tried calling them. Mitch said they probably got arrested."

I shook my head.

"I went by the house, and there were cops everywhere. Mitch said it was because someone ratted us out." Tears welled in his eyes. "Tommy is really dead?"

"Mitch shot them and locked them in the underground container. He took the stash, too."

That last part didn't resonate with Cliff, so I rephrased it slightly.

"He took the stash. He's got all your money. He's getting ready to run."

His eyes narrowed. "And leave me with the kid?" He glanced toward the house.

That part didn't make sense. I figured Wayne Sadler would take the kid.

"Where's Mitch?" I asked.

"He went to the kid's mother's house. He said he had some stuff to discuss with her."

If he was running, could Wayne be going to Alicia Donnelly's house to kill her? For what reason? He already had Patrick. Would killing her stop the police from hunting for her son? No. Then what was the purpose? None of it made sense.

"What's he driving?" I asked.

"His truck." Cliff bent over and cried. "Tommy. Oh, Christ, Tommy."

"Patrick!" I hollered at the house. "Patrick."

The boy came outside. "Did you call the police?"

He nodded.

It was then that I heard them in the distance. Sirens.

Coffey flopped over in the driveway and curled up in the fetal position. I put my hand on Patrick's shoulder. While we waited for the approaching police, we watched a grown man weep for his brother.

Chapter 38

When Patrick and I pulled into Alicia Donnelly's neighborhood, it looked like a law enforcement convention. Ten patrol units were parked haphazardly along her street. The Spokane Police Department, Spokane County Sheriff's Office, and Washington State Patrol were represented.

Smiling law enforcement officers stood about chatting amiably. A couple deputies laughed as they stood near a handcuffed Wayne Sadler, who sat dejectedly on the curb.

On the hood of a patrol car was a handgun. Its slide was locked back, and a clip sat nearby.

"Look at this," a young deputy yelled. Most of us in the vicinity turned his way. He held up a bag of marijuana he'd just found in an old GMC pickup parked in Alicia's driveway.

Sadler glanced over, then dropped his chin back to his chest.

"You won't believe it," the deputy yelled excitedly. "There's a bunch more in here."

A sergeant hurried toward the deputy, no doubt to tell him to stop searching the vehicle. They'd want to get a search warrant to make the seizure unassailable in court.

On the steps to her house, Alicia Donnelly watched the entire proceedings with her arms crossed.

With the boy by my side, Patrick and I were almost at the sidewalk when a mustached deputy held up a hand. "Yo, you two, stay back."

I pointed at Alicia. "That's the boy's mother."

She noticed us and hollered, "Patrick!"

When the deputy glanced back at her, the kid bolted by him. He faced me again. "Well, you stay back."

"Let him by," Alicia shouted.

The deputy rubbed his mustache then jerked his head in the direction of the house.

Alicia hugged Patrick as I walked over. She broke the embrace when I neared. "Thank you, Mr. Cutler." It was unexpected, but she hugged me, too.

I lifted my chin in the direction of Sadler. "What happened?"

"He showed up and wanted in the house. I wouldn't let him. Not without Patrick." She held her son by the shoulder as the boy eyed his father. "He said he had something for me."

I spotted the gun on the hood of the patrol car. Was he coming to kill her?

"He didn't say what he wanted?" I asked.

She shook her head. "He wasn't here but a minute before the police arrived. I can't believe how many got here so quick."

"I called nine-one-one," Patrick said.

"You did?" Alicia asked.

"They arrested Uncle Cliff. It was crazy."

A cluster of deputies drifted toward the truck to check out the rookie's find. Two remained in the street chatting casually. Still sitting alone on the curb was Wayne Sadler.

"Be right back," I muttered, but neither mother nor son seemed to care that I was leaving their conversation.

No one stopped me as I crossed the lawn and stood next to Sadler.

"What were you hoping to do here?" I asked.

He looked up. "Who the fuck are you?"

"A fly in the ointment."

"A what?"

"Were you coming to kill her?"

"You gotta read me my rights."

I squatted but didn't look directly at him. My head swiveled so that I could watch the deputies. "I'm not a cop."

His eyes widened with hope. "Help me escape, and I'll pay you. I got money."

"Tell me why you killed Peyton."

"Who?"

"The old man. You ran over his wife and daughter fifteen years ago."

"Fuck if I did." He glanced around. "Listen, I got fifty grand squirreled away—"

"Say that again."

"I got fifty grand."

"About the old man?"

He smirked. "The old guy bought it, huh? Sounds like someone else got him before me. Same result. Problem solved."

My face hardened, and I wanted to punch him regardless of his handcuffs.

Sadler shrugged. "He deserved what he got. Just wish it could have been me." He glanced around. "About that money."

It didn't make sense. He had to be lying. Had to be. Although, he said he would have if he could have found him.

"What are you doing here?" I asked.

I needed to make sense of his coming to Alicia's so it would help me put the finger on the truth. His story about Peyton wasn't making sense. None of this was making sense.

"What's it matter?" He looked back at Alicia. "Unless you were sticking it to her?"

With her arm around Patrick's shoulder, Alicia turned away from Sadler's gaze.

"Figures," Sadler said. His chin returned to his chest. "Should have known better. Stupid."

I stared at him. Could it have been as simple as that? He bought her a house. Paid for everything Patrick needed. She said he often flirted about them coupling up again. Could Wayne Sadler have still harbored feelings for Alicia Donnelly? Is that why he stayed in town for so long? Did he love her? Had he come here to beg her to run away with him and Patrick?

"Hey!" Both Sadler and I looked up. The mustached deputy was rapidly approaching us. "Get away from him!"

I stood and stepped back.

"What do you think you're doing?"

"Nothing," I said.

"He threatened me," Sadler said half-heartedly.

"You what?" the deputy said.

"He's her boyfriend." His words were filled with grief. "He said he was going to kill me for coming here."

"That's a lie." I lifted my hands. "I never said that."

It didn't matter, though. The next twenty minutes were spent trying to convince a bunch of deputies that I didn't threaten him and that I wasn't, in the words of Wayne Sadler, sticking it to Alicia Donnelly.

Chapter 38

When I finally got home, I walked Corporal to the park and let the big dog run free. Several people watched with amusement as the Shepherd sprinted back and forth. One woman, however, seemed horrified that I let the dog off the leash. She didn't say anything, though. She simply glowered at me then moved to another part of the park.

My thoughts returned to Wayne Sadler.

He was now in custody. They had arrested him on his longstanding warrant. They also charged him with possession of marijuana with intent to distribute and possession of an illegal firearm. They hadn't figured out the intricacies of Patrick's custody situation, so no one felt comfortable charging Sadler with kidnapping at the time. A prosecuting attorney could always charge that later after reviewing the case.

Sadler wasn't charged with the homicides in Deer Park or the two drug dealers. No one on the scene knew about them. Those cases were the responsibility of Detective Ackerman. With Sadler behind bars, the detective could charge the man with those crimes whenever convenient.

I still couldn't shake Sadler's denial of killing Peyton. It bothered me. He had to have done it, I told myself. Was likely to have done it, I corrected myself. Just because a criminal denies wrongdoing doesn't mean it wasn't committed. Sadler would deny killing the men in his crew, the drug dealers, and who knows who else.

Besides, the man said he would have killed Peyton. That might have been a tacit admission. A prosecuting attorney might even use it in a murder trial. Career criminals never own up to anything. They won't even acknowledge pondering a crime, yet Sadler admitted to thinking about killing Peyton.

Why?

And Sadler was openly happy that Peyton was dead. That alone wasn't culpability, but it was something. Did he think it was a perfect crime? Or had he really not been involved? Could I live with the fact that Sadler was caught but refused to own up to Peyton's murder? What other choice did I have?

After the dog tired himself out from racing about, we returned to the Claremont. Once inside my apartment, Corporal lapped up an entire bowl of water then curled into a ball for a nap. The good life.

I reconsidered the two envelopes on the coffee table— the *In Case of Emergency* letter and the one for Erin. I'm not usually a worrier, but if something ever happened to me, the dog should go to someone who at least felt a duty to look after him. I'd mail the letter to Erin in the morning. If I felt the need to say the words before a dangerous situation, I should say them when things were safe.

Sitting on the couch now, the events of the week replayed in my head. I pulled everything apart and tried to look at them like a puzzle. No matter how I put it back together, it always came back to the point of Sadler denying he killed Peyton.

***

A knock on the door caused me to jump. I'd fallen asleep on the couch. The clock showed it to be shortly after ten. Opening the door, I saw the beautiful and unexpected

Tanya Robertson.

"Hey." My voice sounded froggy.

"I saw you on TV."

A news crew arrived at Alicia Donnelly's house and filmed the deputies stuffing Wayne Sadler into the back of a cruiser. Catching a fugitive who had been on the run for fifteen years would make for some good ratings. I'm sure someone in the sheriff's department's administration had alerted the channel to the photo opportunity.

She walked into the apartment. "Did you help catch that guy?"

"Something like that." I shut the door.

"Do you want to talk about it?"

"Not really."

"Okay," she purred and moved toward me. Her arms slid around my waist. "I don't have anywhere to be tonight, so we have—"

I gently grabbed her hands from behind my back and pulled them to the front.

"What's wrong?" she asked.

"I don't want to do this."

Her brow furrowed. "Why?"

"Does it matter?"

"Yes, it matters." She wasn't the type of woman a man said no to very often—if ever. "It most certainly matters."

"I'm only a distraction for you."

She cocked her head. "That's not true. You mean more than that."

"We never go anywhere together. You only come here. I've never been to your place."

"You call me sometimes."

"And you come by if the mood strikes you."

Her face pinched.

"Tanya, you want someone with money, a fancy job, maybe a title. That's not me."

"When did you become such a prude?"

"I'm tired. It's been a long day."

"I'll call you later," she said. "Maybe we can go—"

"No." I shook my head. "It's done. We're done."

"If I walk out …" She pointed at the door.

"I know."

"So that's it? You're just springing this on me?"

"Yeah."

She extended her middle finger and smirked. "That's what I think of this." She thrust the extended finger forward. "What I think of you."

"You're not the only one."

"Damn you." She left the apartment then and didn't bother closing the door. Her heels clicked angrily down the hall. I quietly shut the door and headed toward my bedroom.

Before I even made it to my bed, there was another knock on the door. I considered ignoring it, but there was a second, more earnest knock.

When I opened the door this time, Erika Taylor stood there. Her jaw flexed, and her lips trembled. She blinked several times.

"Want to come in?" I asked.

Erika glanced down the hall. "Who was she?"

"Come inside."

She waited several seconds as if she were considering what coming in might mean. When she finally entered, Corporal got up and walked over. He bumped his head into her hip, and she stroked his fur. "If you think I'm going to cry because of some hoochie, you got me mixed up with another girl."

"Her name is Tanya, and we had a thing."

"*Had?*" Her jaw moved side to side. "She's not your girlfriend?"

"No. Never."

She rolled her lips together. "Never was, but you had a thing?"

I shrugged. "It was complicated."

"And tonight? You and she didn't?"

"No."

"She was pretty. More your type than me."

"Never say that."

She lowered her head and whispered, "Do you like me?" Her voice sounded unsure. Almost, like a little girl. It was a sudden change from the tough girl a moment before.

"I do."

"That's good." Her voice was still soft.

"Is it?"

She looked up. "Don't you think so?"

I smiled and embarrassment flashed across her face.

"I'm sorry," she said. "I can be..." she pretended to struggle for the word, "pushy."

"A little."

The corner of her mouth turned up into a smile. "But you need to be pushed."

"Why do I need to be pushed?"

"You would have never asked me out if I hadn't pushed."

"You said you hadn't been out with a guy in a long time."

"And I hadn't. I might be pushy, but I'm not easy."

"I didn't say that."

"You better not." She came forward then. "You promise that you and her didn't do anything tonight?"

"I promise."

"In that case…" She kissed me then.

"In that case…" She kissed me then.

Chapter 39

Erika stayed until the morning. We fell asleep in each other's arms. Shortly before seven, she kissed me lightly then left. I rolled over and let sleep overwhelm me again. Another hour passed, and I woke up with dog breath in my face. Corporal was more effective than an alarm clock.

"Need to go outside?"

He trotted to the door. I got dressed and grabbed his leash. I considered bringing my gun, but it no longer seemed a necessity with Wayne Sadler in jail. And I couldn't fully be sure it wasn't a stolen gun no matter what Deacon promised.

The dog and I headed to the park. Once off his leash, he made like a maniac and ran for the woods. I was thankful for his modesty since I hadn't brought a bag. If he kept this up, we might have found a compromise to my desire not to pick up after him.

In a moment, he zipped out of the trees and ran around the open area. He would occasionally run by and bump into my legs before darting away. He sprinted like this off and on for a good thirty minutes until he dropped to the grass. That was the signal to head back.

Once back at the Claremont, we entered the elevator and the doors closed. A maintenance man had painted over the previous graffiti, but that didn't stop the vandals. The bare surface provided an opportunity for new crudity.

FUCK This Paint! It don't intimate me, neither.

Geniuses, I thought—all of them.

On the sixth floor, the heavy metal music continued to play from the first apartment. I wondered if its occupant might be responsible for some of the graffiti. I'd never seen him. For all I knew, it could be a woman that lived there. It was unlikely a woman would listen to that kind of music.

Sexist, I thought. My age was showing.

Women had poor taste, just like men. It wasn't only guys showing up at those heavy metal concerts. But if that were to happen, would it kill the entire genre? I smiled at the thought.

The dog and I passed apartment 617—Rosa's. From inside, there was a scream followed by a crash. A man bellowed something that sounded like, "That's what you get." A moment later, there was another enormous crash.

I quickly moved to the door. Corporal must have sensed my anxiety and skittered to the side on the hallway linoleum.

The door was unlocked, and I pushed it open. In the middle of the apartment, standing over the unmoving Rosa, was her boyfriend, Houston. On the floor next to her was a smashed potted plant and a busted TV. The bastard had dropped the television on her.

Houston spun around. His face was beet red, and his lips pulled back from his teeth in a snarl. "I knew it!" He hunched forward and balled his fists. "You're next!"

"Present arms!" I shouted, and Corporal barked. The dog yanked to get free from the leash.

The gnashing of teeth briefly spooked the big man, and he straightened. Houston recovered quickly and said, "Let him go." Hunching now, he grinned menacingly at Corporal. "I dare you. I'll kill it like I did your friend."

I froze.

Like I did your friend.

The revelation stunned me.

All this time, I chased the wrong man.

Houston didn't hesitate, though. He kicked the barking Corporal in the chest. The dog yelped and spiraled back toward me. He grunted as he bounced against my legs. Corporal found his footing, turned, and lunged again. I let go of the leash and yelled, "Fire!"

The dog caught Houston's right arm, and the big man screamed. He tried to jerk free, but that only caused more pain. Houston shrieked. With his free hand, he pummeled the dog.

I moved forward and hit Houston in the face. Then I did it a second time. A third.

Now, the big man didn't know who to strike—the dog or me. He seemed momentarily confused. Rage quickly provided him some clarity, though. He swung a looping haymaker that was thrown off course by the dog hanging from his arm.

With him twisted up, I punched him in the side of the face with a left-right combo that rocked him. He stumbled sideways and tripped over the TV. He collapsed to the floor. Being on his back angered Houston, but it put him at the same level as the dog. He rolled over, and he hammered at Corporal.

The dog yawped and let go.

Houston looked up at me. His face contorted with anger. "Now, it's your—"

I kicked him in the face. He whipped violently back, and the back of his head smacked against the floor. There was no need to check if he was conscious or not. He stopped moving, and his eyes closed. It was too much to hope that I'd killed him.

Before attending to Rosa, I grabbed her phone and dialed 911. When the operator answered, I said, "Claremont apartments, room six one seven. Attempted murder. Start medics. Come quick."

Then I put the phone down and left the line open. Dispatch would record the call until patrol units arrived.

I checked Rosa's pulse. It was weak. Her hair was matted with blood. Her face a pulpy mess.

Corporal moved to the opposite side of the room with his tail down. He stood there and watched. "At ease," I said. The dog turned in a circle before lying with some difficulty.

"Help is on the way," I said to Rosa. I didn't know if she could hear me. I held her hand—both to comfort her and to check her pulse. It was so weak I touched her neck again.

I told the lies suitable in situations like this—everything will be all right, everything will work out okay. I never told her that it wasn't as bad as it looked—that was a lie I couldn't bring myself to utter.

The entire time I sat next to her, I kept a watchful eye on the slumbering Houston. Blood leaked from his mouth, and his arm looked like hamburger. Yet, I still expected him to rise like the villain at the end of my favorite action flicks.

He didn't.

Was it too much to hope the man choked on his blood? Or died of a heart attack? Or asphyxiated from swallowing his tongue?

I stopped with the childish hopes and returned to the meaningless lies. Touching Rosa's neck revealed her pulse had grown fainter.

Heavy footfalls came from down the hall. It sounded as

if the Army had arrived.

"They're here," I said to Rosa and squeezed her hand. "Help is here."

Four cops burst into the room, followed by a couple of medics.

Before I could say anything, one of the cops shouted, "On the ground!"

I tried to protest, but several hands yanked me away from Rosa and spun me to the ground. Facing the dog with my chest on the floor, Corporal started to get up. It looked like a painful rise, and the dog did it out of loyalty and training.

"At ease," I said.

"Shut up," one of the cops grunted. A knee pressed across my shoulders as my right arm was twisted behind my back. A handcuff snapped around my wrist.

Thankful he didn't need to jump into another fray, Corporal settled back into his curl.

"Good dog," I said. "You're a good dog."

My second arm was brought behind my back. The remaining cuff ratcheted into place.

Chapter 40

Friday's newspaper printed Wayne Sadler's arrest in the valley on the front page. It was below the fold, but still front page, nonetheless. A short article in Tuesday's paper detailed his fugitive warrant and the killing of Peyton's wife and daughter. Today's newspaper wrapped everything together. My favorite part was the police chief's crediting Detective Ackerman for cracking the case.

"It was through the tireless work of Detective Gary Ackerman that this fugitive was found," the chief was quoted as saying. "Finding Sadler not only led to the safe return of Patrick Donnelly but the solving of five murders. It also led to the dismantling of a major smuggling ring that brought marijuana in from Canada."

The chief graciously offered some praise to the sheriff's office for their assistance in capturing Sadler, but that was it.

In the regional section, there was an article on Rosa. She died overnight in the hospital where she'd been since the day of her attack. Her boyfriend, Houston Fulkerson, had been arrested in conjunction with the assault. The detective assigned to that case declined to say what new charges would be brought but did say it would likely be "some degree of murder."

I tossed the newspaper to the side when my breakfast arrived—two over-easy eggs, hash browns, and toast.

Peyton Meyers' murder might go unsolved unless Houston Fulkerson copped to it. After the initial officers and medics responded to the scene, a detective came around. The severity of the crime dictated that level of response. I told him Houston said, "I'll kill it like I did your friend." It was an excited utterance and could get beyond the hearsay rule in court, but it was thin to build a murder charge.

Now that Rosa was dead, Houston Fulkerson would be charged with her murder. There was too much evidence, not to mention a witness—me. I suspected the cops—or the prosecutor—would decide that the slam dunk murder charge would have to serve as justice for not just Rosa, but Peyton as well. I wasn't sure I agreed with that idea but didn't expect they'd consult me.

Detective Ackerman also came by to see me. Not only did he want to check in following Wayne Sadler's arrest, but he also heard about the altercation with Houston Fulkerson.

He'd gotten out of the hospital the night of Sadler's capture, but Ackerman mainly looked normal. He had a black eye and a pronounced limp that would both go away with time. The concussion he sustained during the collision was what worried hospital staff enough to keep him for observation.

We chatted for a bit and added up the tolls of both Sadler and Fulkerson. As we did the math, I couldn't help feel as if I were responsible for some of those deaths.

Did my poking into Wayne Sadler's affairs cause him to kill those drug dealers and later his crew members?

And what about Fulkerson? Was it the right thing for Peyton and me to intervene that morning when he was harassing Rosa? Should we have called the cops and let them take care of it? Would Rosa's and Peyton's deaths have been avoided?

I stared at my plate. Broken egg yolks congealed with golden hash browns. The toast had grown cold. I pushed the dish away.

***

That afternoon I finished reading *The Big Sleep*. Corporal lay near my fee. At the end of the book, Raymond Chandler wrote that it doesn't matter where we fall when we die, whether it's in our sleep or at the hands of men like Wayne Sadler or Houston Fulkerson. What matters is how we lived and the loved ones we leave behind.

It was a good story, and thoughts of how we die lingered after I closed the book.

I'm sure it meant I needed to make some life changes, but I didn't know how to start.

***

Erika stopped by before she went to work at the club. After petting the dog, she slipped her arms around me.

"Feeling any better?" she asked.

I nodded.

"I saw the article in the paper today. They didn't mention your name."

"They wouldn't."

"Are you okay with it?"

"Why not?"

"You did most of the work."

"Ackerman has to do the hard part. He has to make the charges stick."

She shrugged. "Hard to pay the rent that way."

I sat on the couch, and Erika moved next to me.

"Bosco's been asking about you."

"That's nice."

"Want me to say anything to him?"

"Like what?"

"Like you're ready to come back."

I eyed the copy of *The Big Sleep* on the coffee table. "I'm not sure I want to."

She stiffened. "You don't?"

"Maybe I want to do something on my own."

"Be an entrepreneur?"

That word didn't fit with my vision. I shrugged. "I'm still figuring it out."

Erika sat quietly for several moments.

"What?" I asked.

"Where does that leave us?"

"How do you mean?"

"If you're not going to work at the club and you want to do your own thing," she moved her finger back and forth between the two of us, "do we have something or not?"

I smiled. "You told me you were pushy."

"Yeah."

"So, push."

Did You Enjoy the Book?

Thank you for reading *Cutler's Chase*. I'm always grateful when a reader takes time out of their day to comment on one of my novels. If you do write a review, please email me and let me know. I'd love to say thanks!

About the Author

Colin Conway is the creator of the 509 Crime Stories, a series of novels set in Eastern Washington with revolving lead characters. They are standalone tales and can be read in any order.

He also created the Cozy Up series which pushes the envelope of the cozy genre. Libby Klein, author of the Poppy McAllister series, says *Cozy Up to Death* is "Not your grandma's cozy."

Colin co-authored the Charlie-316 series. The first novel in the series, *Charlie-316*, is a political/crime thriller that has been described as "riveting and compulsively readable," "the real deal," and "the ultimate ride-along."

He served in the U.S. Army and later was an officer of the Spokane Police Department. He's owned a laundromat, invested in a bar, and run a karate school. Besides writing crime fiction, he is a commercial real estate broker.

Colin lives with his beautiful girlfriend, three wonderful children, and a codependent Vizsla that rules their world.